THE GIRL
WHO STOLE
an ELEPHANT

THE GIRL WHO STOLE an ELEPHANT

NIZRANA FAROOK

nosy crow

First published in the UK in 2020 by Nosy Crow Ltd
The Crow's Nest, 14 Baden Place
Crosby Row, London SE1 1YW

www.nosycrow.com

ISBN: 978 1 78800 634 7

Nosy Crow and associated logos are trademarks and/or registered
trademarks of Nosy Crow Ltd

Text copyright © Nizrana Farook, 2020
Cover copyright © David Dean, 2020

The right of Nizrana Farook to be identified as the author of this
work has been asserted.

Printed and bound in the UK by Clays Ltd, Elcograf S.p.A.
Typeset by Tiger Media

Papers used by Nosy Crow are made from wood grown in
sustainable forests

3 5 7 9 10 8 6 4 2

For Nuha and Sanaa

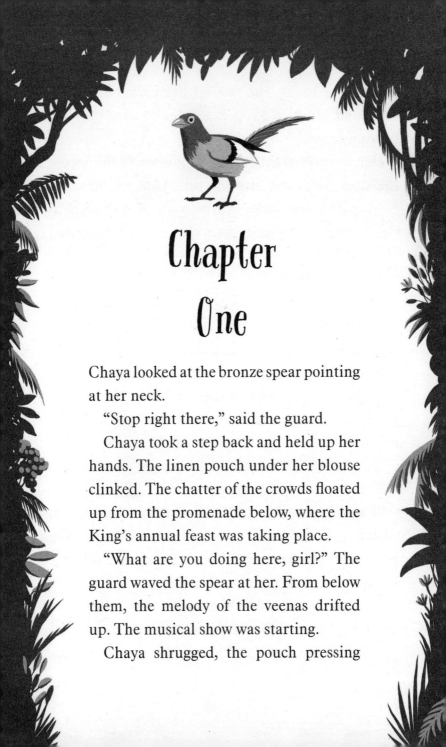

Chapter One

Chaya looked at the bronze spear pointing at her neck.

"Stop right there," said the guard.

Chaya took a step back and held up her hands. The linen pouch under her blouse clinked. The chatter of the crowds floated up from the promenade below, where the King's annual feast was taking place.

"What are you doing here, girl?" The guard waved the spear at her. From below them, the melody of the veenas drifted up. The musical show was starting.

Chaya shrugged, the pouch pressing

against her chest. She rubbed her palms down her skirt and tried to keep her voice level. "I'm just looking around."

Her voice brought two more guards to the top of the stone steps cut into the hill. This was how the royal palace was built – a network of buildings at the top of the mountain, every rock and ledge forming courtyards and pools for the royal household while they ruled from above.

"You're not allowed here," the guard said to Chaya. "You should be down below, enjoying the food and the festivities."

Not Chaya. She much preferred breaking into the Queen's rooms and stealing her jewels. There was a particularly nice blue sapphire in her pouch at that moment.

"Well?" The man jabbed his spear towards her. "What have you got to say for yourself?"

"I wanted to get a little closer to the palace. See what it's like. It looks so pretty from down there." She pointed in the direction of her village and made her face go all wistful.

The guard sighed. "Fine. Just make sure you don't do it again." He put his spear down. "Anything past the lion's entrance is strictly out of bounds to the public."

Chaya looked back and nodded meekly, as if noticing the giant lion statue for the first time, even though it could be seen from villages miles away. The stone stairway carved between the crouching lion's paws led into the complex of buildings that made up the inner palace.

"Come on now." The guard gripped her arm, making her wince. He pulled her to the cobbled walkway sloping downwards towards the celebrations below. "I don't want to see you here again."

The Queen's jewels jangled in her pouch. There were sapphires, tourmalines and star rubies, set in heavy, shiny gold. How many jewels did one person need anyway? And these were just the ones from the drawer in the rosewood table by the bed. Pity she'd had to leave so quickly when she heard voices outside the door. And then to be seen when she was halfway down to the promenade was just bad luck.

She shrugged herself free of the guard and set off, her arm stinging from where his fingers had pinched her.

In spite of everything Chaya found herself gasping at the view from up there. The kingdom of Serendib spread out around her as far as the eye could see, thick green forests and strips of silver rivers, with the King's City below and clusters of little villages beyond.

But she wasn't ready to leave yet. Chaya paused near a tamarind tree and pretended to look up at the monkeys on it. Dappled sunshine prickled her face as she looked at the guard out of the corner of her eye.

He had stopped walking but was still watching her. She heard him swear loudly. "What are you doing now? Get out, girl, before I come and give you a thrashing."

The sensible thing to do was to get out of there as fast as she could. But the Queen's rooms were calling out to her. It was as if she could hear their whisper, right there in the warm sun. The softness of the velvet rugs, the gauzy bed curtains dancing in the breeze, and the promise of more riches within the ebony and teak cabinets.

Suddenly a commotion came from above her, near the Queen's quarters. She heard shouting and the sound of people running.

Chaya thought back quickly. Had she forgotten to close the drawer in her rush?

She sneaked a quick look over her shoulder to see a figure running down the cobbled path behind her.

It really was time to get out.

Chaya carried on walking as casually as she could. Her heart hammered at the sounds behind her.

She was just passing under the stone lion when she heard a yell.

"Hey, you!"

Chaya sped up, her bare feet scorched by the cobbles.

"Hey! I need to talk to you, girl."

She had to get away fast or everything would be over. Her feet slapped harder on the path and her breath came out in puffs.

There was a scuffle of hurrying feet behind her.

Chaya hitched up her skirt and raced down the path. The sound of thundering feet chased her; heavy sandals pounding on cobbles.

She pulled up with a jolt when she saw a row of guards racing towards her from below. She turned and ran blindly sideways, springing up some steps into the Queen's prayer hall and threading through its granite columns. Spears clattered against columns as the guards tramped after her. She got to the far side of the hall and plunged down into the foliage, thrashing through it and down the steps into the formal gardens.

She found herself close to the promenade where the

feast was taking place. The smell of frying sweetmeats meant the food tables were just round the corner.

Chaya skidded to a halt in front of two boys stuffing rice cakes down their shirts. They looked up in alarm at her sudden arrival, and took off in different directions.

Leaping away from them she pitched into a crowd of dancers and musicians. The revellers were oblivious to the unfolding drama, and cymbals clashed and bare-torsoed dancers jumped and twirled to the beat of drums. She ran through the band, clapping her hands over her ears to escape the shrill sounds of the swaying flutes.

"Stop her!" came a shout. "*Stop her!*" The dancers paused, one by one, and some of the music petered out. People gawped, looking behind Chaya towards the guards chasing her. "The girl! *Stop the girl!*"

A man in the crowd lunged at Chaya but she slipped out of his grasp and ran towards the gates of the royal complex. Coconut-flower decorations tied along strings came crashing down as she ran through them, wrapping themselves around her like a trap. She tore them off and kept running.

Elephants from the temple stood on the lawn ahead of her, draped in their mirror-studded regalia, ready for the pageant later. In the middle of them stood the King's Grand Tusker himself, Ananda. He was wearing his special maroon and gold garments, and his tusks were massive and powerful up close.

Chaya ground to a stop on the grass and looked back. She was boxed in.

She sprinted up and ducked under the mighty bulk of Ananda, the world instantly going dark and dank. His mahout gave a shout and grabbed at her plait, yanking her head back, but she broke free and rolled out on the other side. She sprang up to see the mahout turn and yell at the guards thundering towards them, as some of the elephants had started to toss their heads alarmingly.

"Stop!" The mahout waved his arms at the guards. "The elephants are getting disturbed."

The guards slowed down and Chaya took her chance. She ran to the boundary and dashed out through the gates. She was free.

Skirting the city, she headed towards the patches of wilderness on the east side of the palace, the wind flying through her hair as she sprinted away.

When she got there she stopped and leaned against a tree, catching her breath. She peered through the wilderness and smiled.

She'd lost them.

Chaya shimmied up the tree, hands scratching against the rough bark. She settled herself in one of the high branches and picked out the coconut blossoms stuck in her hair. Lifting her linen pouch over her neck, she dropped the jewels into her lap. They sparkled in shards of bright blue, green and pink against the grey of her skirt.

It had been a huge risk. Her boldest robbery to date. And yet she'd pulled it off.

She picked a *jambu* fruit from a branch nearby and crunched into its juicy pink flesh, peering through the leaves at the royal compound in the distance.

It was pandemonium down there. The crowds were scattered and panicked, clusters of people moving in different directions. The King, standing out in his gold-encrusted waistcoat, had come down from the dais and was roaring at his staff. The Queen and her procession of ladies were being guided out of the promenade up to the palace. The mahouts on the green were trying desperately to calm their confused charges and stop them running amok. In the middle of it all, Ananda lifted up his majestic head and trumpeted loudly into the blue, blue sky.

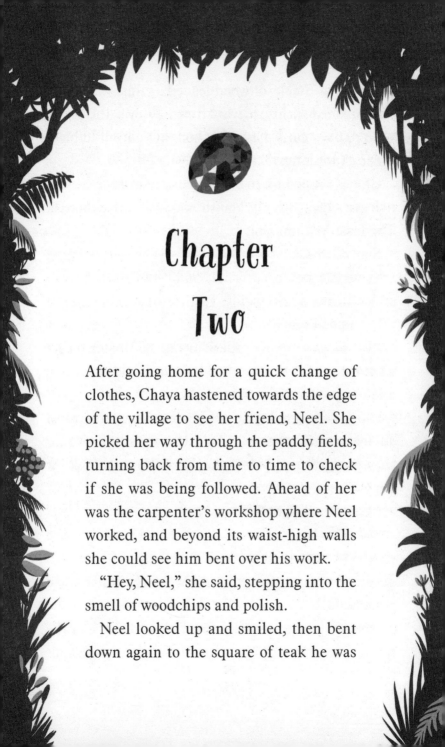

Chapter Two

After going home for a quick change of clothes, Chaya hastened towards the edge of the village to see her friend, Neel. She picked her way through the paddy fields, turning back from time to time to check if she was being followed. Ahead of her was the carpenter's workshop where Neel worked, and beyond its waist-high walls she could see him bent over his work.

"Hey, Neel," she said, stepping into the smell of woodchips and polish.

Neel looked up and smiled, then bent down again to the square of teak he was working on. Stacks of wood leaned against walls, and half-finished furniture was strewn all over the place. "You're back early, Chaya. I thought you would be at the feast for longer."

Chaya slipped on to a stool next to him. "I … had to leave a bit suddenly. You should have come though. The feast was amazing."

She peered over the half-walls. The surrounding area was deserted as usual, and only a soft breeze swept through the paddy, rustling the underside of the thatched roof.

"We have so many orders to finish. Master didn't want me to go." Neel worked his chisel into the wood, and brown shavings fell at his feet.

Chaya wondered what was happening at the royal palace at that moment. She'd lost them, but would they just give up? Surely they'd continue to look for her?

"Are you all right?" asked Neel.

"Me? Yeah. Of course." She pointed to the square of wood he was working on. "That looks different. All geometric patterns instead of the swirly designs you usually do."

"Oh, this is something we're making for one of the foreign merchants. There's a new spice merchant in town and it looks like he's here for good. Their patterns are all like this. I had to use a ruler…"

Chaya zoned out as Neel talked. How long would the King's men look for her? They wouldn't give up easily. Her head snapped back at a thwacking noise. But it was only a crow hopping along the top of the wall.

"OK, Chaya, what's going on?" Neel put down the chisel and stared at her.

"What do you mean?"

"You're all jumpy. What's happened?"

"You're not going to like it."

"Tell me anyway."

"It's … the usual."

Neel sighed. "And what's it for this time?"

"It's Vijay, one of the boys at the river. He was attacked by a crocodile when he was swimming. I was there when it happened."

"Yes, you told me. What can you do for him now, though?" Neel blew on the piece of wood, puffing out a cloud of brown dust into the air.

Chaya rubbed her nose. "His family has been told of a medicine man that can fix him, and he might be able to walk again. But they need a lot of money very quickly. They have to hire a cart for the three-day journey, and then there's payment for the months of treatment, of course."

Neel shook his head. "I don't know if I should admire you or think you're completely mad."

"This time, you might be right to say mad."

"Why, what's different?"

"Like I said, they need a *lot* of money. I might have taken something … more valuable than usual."

Neel stared at her. "Which is?"

Chaya undid the pouch and the jewels spilled out. They clattered on to the intricate carving Neel was working on, lodging in various grooves. The sapphire shone the bluest of blues, but a sparkling pink ruby was a close second, with a silvery star shimmering inside it.

Neel shrank back as if he'd been stung. "Chaya, *what on earth?* Where did you get those from?"

She picked up the sapphire and held it to the light. "The Queen's bedside table."

Neel looked at the jewels, and back at Chaya. "Please tell me you're joking."

"It's not so bad." Chaya put the sapphire back with the other jewels. Neel was always such a worrier, he made things seem worse than they were. "I don't think they recognised me."

"Wait a minute, *someone saw you?*"

"Calm down, Neel. I ran away. I'm safe."

"*Calm down?* This isn't like stealing a few coins here and there. This is the *King* we're talking about."

"Queen, actually." Neel glared at her so she quickly carried on. "Don't you want Vijay to get better? If he's not treated he'll lose his leg. He'll *never* walk again. And anyway, there's someone else who could use some of it too."

"Who?"

"You."

"*Me?*"

"Your parents could have the money so you don't need to work. You're thirteen, Neel. You should come back to school."

"I've told you enough times. I'm fine. I don't need any charity."

"Just hear me out. Not just school, you could even learn Sanskrit and the sciences at the temple. You could have a better life."

"A better life? Or *your* life, you mean."

Chaya threw up her hands. "Fine. So I might have gone a bit too far, stealing from the Queen." She noticed Neel's expression. "OK, a *lot* too far. But I had to find a lot of money, *right away*, while they can still treat Vijay." She gathered the jewels up into the pouch. "I need to get these to his family. They'll leave tonight."

"Wait, Chaya. Think. How's a poor farmer going to sell the Queen's jewels? And what happened? You said someone saw you."

She hoisted the pouch back over her neck. "Oh, it was just one of the guards. He chased me down to the promenade, and other people tried to get me too. It got a bit … manic. But I got away."

"So now they're *looking* for you?"

"Yes, maybe. Oh, no need to look so horrified! I'll give Vijay's mother one piece that she can sell on the journey, far away from here. I'm going to hide the rest at home."

"The King's men are probably searching the villages right now. Don't go *anywhere* with those things on you. We need to hide them at once."

"Hide them? Here?" Chaya's eyes swept round the room. High shelves lined the far wall of the workshop, filled with tools, pots of polish and wooden trinkets. "Everything's so open. What about that box you showed me the other day? The one you made with the hidden compartment. You still got it?"

"Yes. Yes, it's here somewhere." Neel went to

the shelves and hunted through them. He brought down a small box carved with a two-headed bird carrying a snake in its claws. He opened the lid and lifted out a drawer, and after some fiddling about unlocked a secret compartment at the bottom of the box.

Chaya emptied the jewels inside, first taking out a tiny cat's-eye pendant and leaving it aside. Scooping up some wood dust swept into a pile in the corner, she packed it in tightly with the jewels. Neel snapped everything shut and put the box back on a shelf among a few others.

"It's all right," he said, as if guessing what she was thinking. "The master takes these every three months to Galle, and he's only just been, so they're safe."

"Good. This'll blow over soon. I can get them back then." Chaya hoped that was true. She unpicked a few stitches in the hem of her skirt and pushed the cat's-eye pendant in. "I'll give this to Vijay's mother now."

"Fine, but go home straight after. I'll head into the city and see what the talk is. You'll be safe once you're home. Your father—" Neel stopped, looking troubled.

"What? What about Father?"

"Oh, Chaya. If they ever find out you took the jewels

your father will be in big trouble."

"But Father's only a minor official to the King. Why would they blame him?" But even as she said it, realisation slowly dawned.

"He's the village headman! He knows the palace. Layout, access, that kind of thing. They'll think he set it up. They'll never believe a girl did this on her own. And you know what the King is like in a rage. He will have your father—" Neel's eyes darted away from Chaya. "Come on. You need to go home now."

Chaya followed Neel out, with a backwards glance at the box on the shelf. The Queen's pendant brushed her ankle through her hem.

Father.

Had she accidentally put him in danger?

Neel's unfinished sentence couldn't have been any clearer to her.

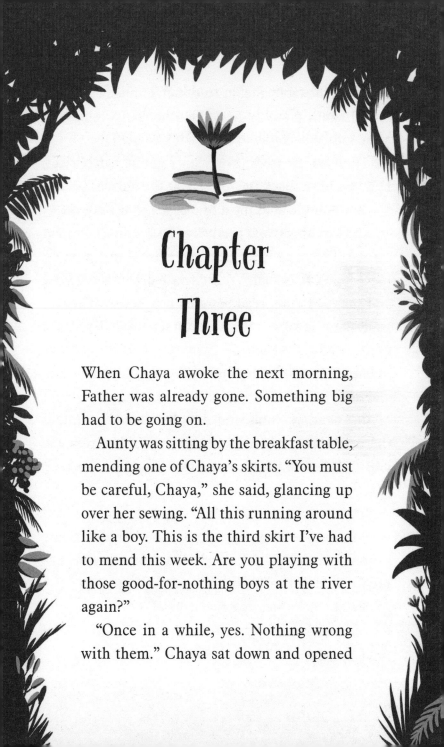

Chapter Three

When Chaya awoke the next morning, Father was already gone. Something big had to be going on.

Aunty was sitting by the breakfast table, mending one of Chaya's skirts. "You must be careful, Chaya," she said, glancing up over her sewing. "All this running around like a boy. This is the third skirt I've had to mend this week. Are you playing with those good-for-nothing boys at the river again?"

"Once in a while, yes. Nothing wrong with them." Chaya sat down and opened a dish on the table. Steam rose from chunks of freshly boiled sweet potato. She helped herself to one with some grated coconut. "Father's left early?"

"There's some trouble brewing right here in Nirissa. Did you hear about the robbery at the palace?"

Chaya nodded, taking a bite of her sweet potato.

"I heard things were pretty bad last night in the next village. The King is furious, and he's taking it out on the people. As usual." Aunty pulled her needle out and snapped the thread between her teeth. "Whoever stole those jewels… It's a death sentence if you ask me."

The food went floury and heavy in Chaya's mouth, and she had difficulty swallowing. She stared out of the window. Sunshine dappled the lawn under the neem tree, where a mongoose slunk across the grass. "Who are they looking for? Do they have a, er, description or something?"

"It's strange, but nobody's sure." Aunty crinkled her brow as she folded up the skirt on her lap. "Some people mention a dark, reedy boy. Some say he was plump, and ran with a limp."

The two boys stealing rice cakes! They'd run away too, and each might have been mistaken as the jewel thief.

"A guard at the palace has even got it into his head that it was a *girl*," said Aunty. "Around twelve years old, medium-brown complexion, hair in a long plait, tall."

"Oh." Chaya studied her mottled reflection on the panelling of the window. "That could be anyone. Even me, for example."

Aunty laughed. "True. Nobody believes him, of course. A girl!"

"What's the trouble they're expecting today then, Aunty?"

"General Siri and his men have been marching through the surrounding villages trying to … *persuade* people to give up the thief. This morning it's our turn, unfortunately."

Chaya blanched at the sound of General Siri's *persuading*. "How long are they going to do that for? If no one confesses they'll have to give up surely?"

"Give up! The King has enemies who'd be glad to see him toppled. You know how paranoid he is about his position. This is huge, someone getting into the palace like that. He's not going to let it go."

Chaya's mouth suddenly felt parched. She poured out a tumbler of water from the clay pitcher.

"What's the matter?" said Aunty. "Why aren't you eating?"

Chaya looked down. The sight of the food made her feel sick. "I'm just not hungry." She pushed her plate away.

Aunty tutted but said nothing.

"I should get going," Chaya said.

"*Chaya*, you've hardly eaten. There's still time before school. Finish your breakfast."

"I want to go and see Neel first." She got up and swung her satchel on to her shoulder.

"That boy Neelan, doesn't he have enough work to do without you always dropping in? My brother spoils you, letting you run around like a wild thing. Other girls of twelve have even stopped going to school by now."

"See you later, Aunty." Chaya hurried past before she could say any more, and hotfooted it out of the house.

Something was wrong in Nirissa.

Where was everyone? The lanes were quiet as Chaya made her way to the workshop. No sounds of *ekel* brooms sweeping out front yards, no metal buckets clanking into wells or the gush of water pouring over bathers.

Shouts echoed in the distance. Chaya ran down the pebbly paths towards them, her satchel slapping against her leg. A dense knot of people blocked the view.

Chaya pushed her way to the front.

The King's men were here.

They were outside one of the little houses. The front door was open and the family's possessions had been thrown outside. Chaya recognised the house. It was Bala's, from school.

A soldier tossed a small sack of rice out of the house, spilling the contents on the ground over a heap of reed mats, pillows, and clothes spotted with lentils. A woman threw herself on the rice, sobbing, and tried to scoop it up with her hands.

No, no, *no*. This couldn't be happening.

General Siri was standing by his horse, dressed in his high-shouldered purple jacket, an embossed-leather dagger sheath strung at his side. Father was next to him and they seemed to be arguing, Father jabbing his arm towards Bala's house. General Siri sighed and turned away.

"You'll all be next," he yelled at the silent crowd. "All of you. Unless you give up the thief."

A whisper passed through the mass of people, and Chaya slipped away. Out of sight of the villagers, and Father, and Bala's family's pain. She leaned against a wattle and daub wall, grinding her head into its roughness.

All this suffering in her village. It was her fault.

A boy's voice screamed. "It wasn't me! It really wasn't."

Chaya squeezed her eyes shut, blocking out the sound of Bala's screaming. She wiped the sweat off her face. She had to do something.

There was a movement in front of her. A small girl was studying Chaya, thumb in mouth. It was Bala's little sister.

"I'm sorry," Chaya whispered. "I'm so sorry. I'll put it right, I promise."

The child glanced round, wondering if Chaya was talking to her.

Chaya stumbled away from the noise and the crowds towards the edge of the village. She broke into a run and bolted down the paths, branches scraping at her arms and snagging on her skirt. She couldn't let this happen. It had to stop.

She flew out of the village and through the paddy fields. Up ahead she could see movement inside the workshop. Neel was there already.

"Neel!" Chaya shouted as she sprinted up. "Neel, I have to give them back."

She held her aching side and halted at the doorway, doubled up and panting.

Neel was standing very stiffly, glaring at her. There were people in the workshop. Customers.

Neel's master, Kumar the carpenter, was with them. He turned to Chaya, frowning slightly, before going back to his customers.

They were a finely dressed merchant and a girl around Chaya's age, probably his daughter. Chaya gawped at their flowing, silken clothes.

"It is perfect," said the merchant, bending over a small cabinet. He spoke his words slowly, Chaya's language sounding strange on his tongue.

Chaya turned back to Neel. There were beads of sweat on his forehead. *What's wrong?* she mouthed. Neel's eyes darted to the girl.

"I'll bring it to you as soon as it's done," said the carpenter. "I'm glad you're satisfied with how it's going."

The merchant nodded and smiled. Thankfully, it looked like they were leaving. The girl turned around.

She was carrying something in her hands.

Chaya gasped. She clutched Neel, whose arm was hot and clammy.

"We will take this," said the girl.

She held up a box. It was carved with a two-headed bird, carrying a snake in its claws.

Chapter Four

The box seemed to mock Chaya from the girl's hands. She felt like snatching it off her right there and then.

The merchant frowned at the two-headed bird on the lid. "That's an odd-looking carving. Choose something else, Nour."

Chaya sprang at Nour and gripped the box, her hands tight on the smooth, varnished wood. "Your father's right, this one's really ugly. Look, there are nicer boxes over there."

But Nour wouldn't let go, holding on in

spite of Chaya's efforts. "Sorry," she said, her voice soft and firm at the same time. "I like *this* one."

"Actually, that box is someone else's," said Neel. "I've already promised it. I have to deliver it later today."

The carpenter stared at Neel. "You taking orders for me now, boy? Keep your mouth shut." He swiped his hand to make Neel step away.

"It's a shame you like this particular one, though," said Chaya, still holding tight. "It has a, er, defect."

"That's true," said Neel, nodding from where he had retreated to behind a mahogany cabinet. "The little drawer keeps getting stuck."

"Oh, we don't want it then," said the merchant.

"Yes, we do, Father." Nour tugged at the box. "I like it."

"Not to worry then," said Chaya. "It's easily fixable. Neel will work on it and bring it to you tomorrow."

"I don't mind really," said Nour, taking a hand off to slide the drawer open and shut repeatedly. It looked like it was gliding on oil.

"But I insist," said Neel. "That's not accept—"

"Neelan!" said the carpenter. "Enough. What's the meaning of this? Know your place, boy. Miss Chaya, you'd better leave. And you, boy, another word from you…" He glared at Neel.

Chaya backed out of the workshop, feeling Nour's eyes boring into her all the way. She hesitated in the doorway.

The merchant's expression furrowed as he looked from the carpenter to Neel to Chaya. "Nour, why not take something else? Look, this one has a lotus flower. It looks much nicer."

Chaya nodded to herself. *Yes, put your foot down, Nour's father.* What a spoilt child that Nour was.

"But this one's nicer, I like the pattern. And it's also…" Nour's eyes darted to Chaya, and there was a faint smirk on her face. "It's also heavier than the others." She turned back to the carpenter. "We'll take it."

Chaya watched from behind a clump of papaya trees. A breeze whistled through the trees, blowing wisps of hair into her eyes and whipping at her plait. She had retreated from the workshop but watched, hands on head, as her precious jewels were being taken away.

The merchant stepped outside. Nour followed behind, her floaty red gown swishing through the green of the paddy field. They threaded their way along the path, Nour holding the box like a prize in her hands.

She wouldn't work it out, would she? Neel's handiwork had to be too clever for her. The thought of the jewels being discovered was too much to bear.

The merchant passed Chaya first, talking to Nour over his shoulder in a foreign tongue. He was quite unlike his daughter, big and broad shouldered, with a swarthy face under his white turban in the style of their people. Nour tripped along after him, leaving a smell of warm sand and jasmine behind her.

At the edge of the fields a carriage waited, and Nour got in, followed by her father. They left by the cartway skirting the village towards the King's City. Chaya watched them go before sprinting along the river path. It was a shortcut she'd taken many times, through thorny shrubs that ripped her skirt. She'd just have to face Aunty's wrath later.

Stopping outside the gates into the city, Chaya crept up behind the old war bell. The trundle of wheels followed shortly after, and Nour and her father swept in through the entryway. Chaya followed at a leisurely pace, as she'd seen the carriage stop at the market and Nour get down at a lace stall. The seller measured out and bundled several lengths into fat rounds for Nour. Then she got back in the carriage and they moved on again, taking the little bridge over the lotus-speckled river to the residential part of the city.

This was where all the big villas were, standing in gardens of shady trees thick with frangipani flowers. The carriage turned into a street and stopped at a large house at the end.

So this was where Nour lived. More importantly, this was where the box was going to be.

Not for long, though. Because Chaya was going to get it back.

She smiled from her position behind the wall as Nour took the box inside.

Chapter Five

The next day Chaya sat on a park bench, watching the merchant's house. The stone seat felt cool under her at this time of the morning, and a myna bird twittered on the frangipani branch overhead.

The merchant went out soon after, striding away towards the market. But the sun was high in the sky before Nour came out. She was accompanied by a round-faced woman with a headscarf tied under her chin, who waddled down the street arm in arm with her.

Finally! Chaya sped up the street

towards the house after giving Nour a good five minutes to get away. Chaya was dressed in her usual thieving get-up – a set of ragged old clothes she kept hidden from Aunty in a drawer. It was surprising how invisible poor people were. Nobody ever noticed Chaya when she was dressed like this.

The villa was a typical rich person's house. Large and single-storeyed, with a verandah twice the size of Chaya's, filled with dark, heavy furniture. One look at the house and Chaya knew this was going to be *easy*.

The gate was open but there was a man watering the garden. No problem, front entrances were the most guarded part of a house anyway. Same with the back; always a gaggle of servants chatting there. She wasn't going to enter through either of them.

Chaya headed to the side of the house, which was partly covered by a mound of tall bushes. Just as she'd thought. This side wasn't overlooked from the street. She stood for a minute, casually checking to see if anyone was around, then ran up and leapt on to the window ledge.

She wasn't going to get in through the window, oh no. People were careful with windows – that's how thieves got in. She reached up to the roof and hooked one foot over, hauling herself up.

The roof tiles were scorching under her bare feet as she tiptoed her way across, careful not to dislodge anything. Voices came from the back of the property. She got to the middle of the house, and there it was. The weak point of every rich man's villa: the courtyard.

Chaya lay flat on the roof and peered down into the house, squinting till her eyes adjusted to the light. A well-tended garden with sprays of pink bougainvillea lay at the centre, edged with thin pillars holding up the roof of the inner verandah. A servant girl cleared crockery from a small table set with a bench. No one else was in sight.

Chaya watched the girl leave, cups and saucers clinking on a tray, then dropped down into the garden, landing lightly on the spongy grass.

The girl was walking away down a wide corridor. Chaya rolled over and stepped behind a brass standing lamp. She heard the clinking stop, and sensed the girl turn back to look. People never noticed anything when you were still. What they *did* notice was movement. Chaya stood motionless, imagining the girl's puzzled face looking in her direction. A clock ticked somewhere, counting out the seconds. The tray clinked again as the girl went on her way.

Chaya stole out and pushed open a highly polished

door set with a brass ring for a handle. Inside was a four-poster bed and rich maroon furnishings. A tapestry on the wall had a pattern like the one Neel had been working on, all geometric shapes laid out in stars and triangles. On a stand was a blue-edged length of cloth that was the turban the merchant had worn yesterday. Chaya tiptoed back out.

The next door was open, a patterned curtain fluttering across it. This was a sitting room, with low couches arranged around a big woven rug. This wasn't the room she wanted either.

As she brushed her way through the curtain a man walked towards her, fiddling with an incense burner. Chaya nipped back behind the curtain. She was conscious of her feet showing underneath, but stayed still to avoid the flash of movement. She stiffened as the man passed on the other side, so close she could smell the bitterness of betel on his breath. His footsteps receded towards the back of the house.

Chaya crept out to the adjoining corridor. It led to a dining area with tall windows at the end. A delicious smell came from a tray on the sideboard near her. She lifted up the fly cover on it. There was some kind of fried sweet, coated with powdered sugar, still warm and smelling of syrup. Her mouth watered and fingers itched to pop one in her mouth.

She dropped back the cover and crept out. She was crossing the courtyard to the rooms on the other side when she heard footsteps.

The servant girl was back.

Chaya shimmied up the nearest pillar. She wrapped her legs around the top of the pillar, splayed on the ceiling like a gecko, hands gripping the roof gutter for support.

That was another thing about people. They never looked up.

She was stretched to the maximum, her arm muscles thrumming with the strain. The servant girl was right underneath, taking her time with the crockery. She hummed a tune and laid cups and spoons daintily on a tray.

Chink, chink.

Chaya's arms and hips were on fire.

Chink, chink.

She breathed in and out slowly, willing herself to hold on.

Chink, chink.

Oh, how long was the silly fool going to take?

Chink, chink.

She was going to fall. She couldn't hold on any

more. Her body started to sag, and she fought to grip the gutter with her sweaty fingertips.

The servant girl left, still humming her tune.

Chaya dropped down and leaned on the pillar, catching her breath and massaging her aching arms. There was no time to lose. She bounded up to a panelled door across the courtyard and pushed it open. The first thing that hit her was the smell of jasmine.

She'd found Nour's room.

It had a smaller four-poster bed, with a steamer trunk at the foot of it. A painting of a woman quite like Nour hung on a wall. On the dressing table were hairbrushes and scent bottles, but right in the middle was Neel's wooden box.

Chaya rushed over to it and snatched it up. Finally this nightmare could end. The two-headed bird etching shone softly on the varnished lid as she opened it and fiddled with the secret catch.

A sound of cartwheels startled her as a carriage crunched to a halt outside the house. Chaya snapped the lid shut. There was no time; she had to get out. She'd open it at home. She closed the door softly behind her as she padded back to the courtyard.

A high-pitched scream made Chaya freeze.

The servant girl was standing at the table, her infernal tray in her hand, staring at Chaya. She had come back for a single cup that she'd left on the table, the silly idiot.

The house stirred to attention, as voices and footsteps hurried towards them.

"Sorry, sorry, I'm leaving," Chaya said to the girl. She had no intention of meeting the rest of the household. She threw the box in a high arc on to the roof, where it landed with a crash, sending a tile sliding down. Chaya leapt up and grabbed on to the gutter, swinging for a moment before pulling herself up to the roof.

She plucked the box from where it had fallen and scrammed. She slid down the rest of the roof, tiles scouring the backs of her legs. At the lip she plummeted down and landed on her feet by the side of the house. Behind her, a back gate clattered open and footsteps scuffled in Chaya's direction.

She ran for it. Down the city streets and through the market she went, zigzagging past mounds of *ambarella* fruit and cane-basket displays and sacks of cardamom and cumin. Then out of the city and past the old war bell and its crumbled-down plinth, until she was sure she wasn't being pursued any more.

At home, she went straight to her room to change and hide the box before Aunty saw her. She shut the door and flopped down on the bed, hugging the box to her. The thought of Nour's face when she got home and saw the box gone made her laugh. Served Nour right for trying to mess with her!

The lid had come loose but otherwise the box was fine. Chaya tapped and prodded it the way Neel had shown her, until she heard the click that released the hidden compartment. She took out the drawer and saw the dark shapes nestling among the wood dust.

She lifted out one of them, leaving a trail of wood dust on her bed sheet.

"*No!*" Chaya yelled. She turned the box over and shook the contents out, dumping a dusty mound of pebbles on to her bed.

No. *No*. NO! The thief. *The horrible thief!* Chaya scrabbled in the wood dust for the jewels, but all she found was pebbles.

Every single one of the Queen's jewels was gone.

Her fingers closed on a scrap of paper among the wood dust. She shook it off. It was a note. A very short one.

Nice try.

– Nour

Chapter Six

"Can you *believe it*? How dare she!" Chaya paced the workshop. Her throat felt tight and she pummelled her thighs with her fists. What a nightmare. Where on earth were the jewels?

Neel slumped at his work table, his forehead resting on his hands. It was a good thing Kumar the carpenter wasn't in again – Neel wasn't even bothering with his work today.

"Maybe," he said, his voice muffled as he looked down at the table. "Maybe they're safe now that they're with her."

"Safe! Maybe the jewels are safe, but what about the people? It's so awful, Neel." Chaya flopped against a half-built wardrobe, the shelves digging into her back. "General Siri's still harassing the villagers. He won't give up. He wants a confession."

Neel fingered the note. "I don't understand why she's taken them. Her father is Cassim the merchant. They're rich, aren't they?"

"How did she find out how to open it in *one* night?" said Chaya, stalking around the workshop. "How did she even work out there *was* a secret compartment? Ridiculous – she can't be that clever. Thinks she can outwit us. No *way*."

Neel shook his head. "It doesn't matter. She must have guessed something was up from the way we were acting. And she did say the box felt heavy. The question is, what do we do now?"

"We've got to—" Chaya's mouth dropped open as she saw a slim figure dressed in red walking through the paddy fields towards them.

Of all the *nerve*.

"Neel," she said, her eyes on the figure. "Neel. It's her."

Neel's head whipped up.

Nour stepped gingerly through the fields, her eyes

on the ground. She came into the workshop and stopped in front of them, hands on her hips.

"Where is my box?" she said. "I want it back."

"Where are our *jewels*?" said Chaya, leaning over the table. "Thief."

"Chaya—" began Neel.

Nour laughed. "May I remind you that it wasn't me who broke into somebody's house and stole things?"

"That's different," said Chaya. "I was taking back what was ours."

Neel held up his hand. "Listen—"

"Ours?" Nour snorted. "Really? I bet the *King* would beg to differ."

There was a silence in the workshop.

She knew. Nour knew everything.

"Miss Nour." Neel stood up. "Please. It's not how you think. We need the jewels because of what General Siri's doing to the villagers. We have to give them back and save our people."

"That's not the only reason!" snapped Chaya. "We also want them because they're ours, not *hers*." She glared at Nour before turning back to Neel. "And stop calling her Miss! She's not better than you in any way."

"Chaya, be quiet. I'm sure we can discuss this calm—"

"She should have just stayed out of it," said Chaya, jabbing a finger at Nour. The girl had put them all in danger with her silliness. "Poking her nose into other people's business. Taking what's not hers."

"Hey." Nour threw up her hands. "I *bought* the box."

"Well, the price didn't include the jewels," said Chaya. "So you can't have them."

"Who said I wanted them?" Nour looked scornful. "I only want my box, not the Queen's jewels. *I'm* not a thief." She took a drawstring bag out of her pocket and flung it on the table. "Which is more than I can say for the pair of you."

Chaya stared at the little bag. Neel snatched it up and pulled it open. The sound of jewels clinking together made Chaya's heart soar.

"Thank you so much, Miss Nour. Thank you for understanding," said Neel.

"Neel, she's not doing us a favour! The jewels aren't hers to give away."

"Of course I'm doing you a favour," said Nour. "I mean, I could tell my father, if you like?"

"Oh no, Miss Nour, please don't do that," said Neel. "I'll make sure I get you your box. Actually..." He went up to the shelves and moved some trinkets to the front. "Please choose any one you want. Or two, three, whatever."

Nour stepped around the work table to the shelves.

Chaya marched after her. "Wait a minute, *wait a minute*. Neel, what's this about two or three?"

Neel closed his eyes. "Chaya, I'm *begging* you—"

"But then *you'll* have to pay your master with your wages. As it is he pays you so little."

Nour ignored them and rummaged on the shelves.

"Stop it," Neel hissed at Chaya. "We got the jewels. Don't ruin it now."

Someone cleared their throat behind them. Chaya turned around to see two men had walked into the workshop. They were dressed in identical guard uniforms, and they stamped their shoes on the coir rug, looking around with interest.

Behind them some more people followed through the fields. And in the distance beyond the paddy fields Chaya could see a group of riders on horseback. The ground listed under her feet as a wave of dizziness swept through her.

It was the King's men.

"We're just searching the area," said one of the guards who'd come in, nodding respectfully at Chaya and Nour. "If you two will wait outside?"

"Hey," said the other to Neel. "You, boy. What's that you hid on the shelf there?"

"Nothing," said Chaya. "He works here. His master, Kumar the carpenter, is away. You should come back another time."

Some of the rest of the group approached the workshop.

"Get General Siri," said the man who shouted at Neel. "Something's going on here."

There was a sudden rush of movement. Chaya swung round. Four men surrounded Neel, and one was rummaging around on the shelf. Nour stepped forward and tried to say something, but froze as the man swept his spear back and forth among the wooden knick-knacks, knocking things over and sending them crashing to the floor.

"Stop it!" shouted Chaya. But her voice was drowned out by the clatter of falling wood as item after item of Neel's hard work smashed on the floor.

A swarm of the King's men crowded around the workshop, almost blocking out the light. Soon General Siri himself was at the doorstep, one corner of his lip pinned back in a permanent sneer.

"What do we have here?" His voice was hoarse

and broken.

"The carpenter's away," said Chaya. "You should come back when he's in. Your men have done enough damage here."

General Siri's eyes swept round the workshop. "I don't think so. We'll continue to search it now."

"But the owner isn't in." Chaya stepped up to the doorway and blocked the entrance. "I insist that you come back another time."

General Siri laughed indulgently. "Whoever you are, miss, out of the way now."

"General Siri," said a voice behind Chaya. "Sir. The boy hid something as we came in. We found it."

Chaya turned to see the man hold out Nour's drawstring bag. General Siri took it in his dry, cracked hands, and fear slashed deep into Chaya's heart.

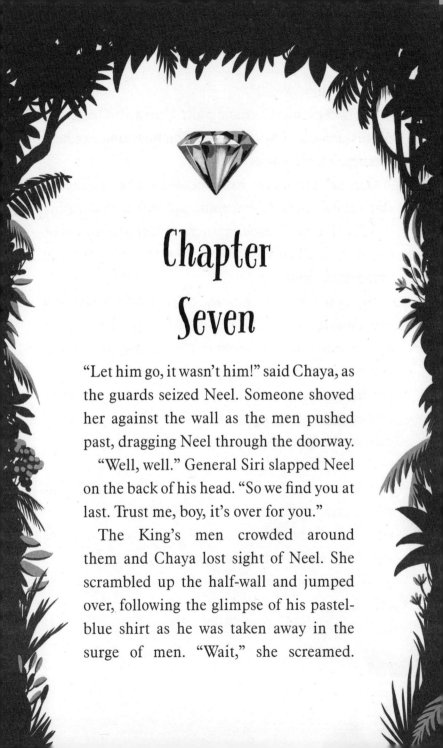

Chapter Seven

"Let him go, it wasn't him!" said Chaya, as the guards seized Neel. Someone shoved her against the wall as the men pushed past, dragging Neel through the doorway.

"Well, well." General Siri slapped Neel on the back of his head. "So we find you at last. Trust me, boy, it's over for you."

The King's men crowded around them and Chaya lost sight of Neel. She scrambled up the half-wall and jumped over, following the glimpse of his pastel-blue shirt as he was taken away in the surge of men. "Wait," she screamed.

"It wasn't him! Wait!"

A guard grabbed her and pulled her away. "Stay out of this, miss." Chaya struggled against him, her hair catching in his copper buttons.

"Let me go." Chaya hit out at the guard. She heard the crack of bone on bone and saw blood pool on his lips, leaving her knuckles stinging. She slipped out of his grasp and ran towards the front, fighting her way through the throng of men.

"It wasn't him. It was *me*. *Me*." Chaya's screams burned her throat, but no one took any notice. She saw two men at the front haul Neel into a cart. Bodies hit against her, buffeting her from side to side, and her ears rang with the whinnying of horses and crunch of cartwheels.

Something scraped against her arm, leaving a slash of blood. She thrust her way to the front, where the purple waistcoat of General Siri flashed golden at the seams, sitting high on his horse. Chaya threw herself in front of him, blocking the way. The horse reared up and General Siri gaped down at her.

"What the—! Get out of the way before you get killed, idiot."

"It was me!" yelled Chaya. "I stole the jewels. It wasn't Neel."

General Siri looked confusedly at his deputy next to him. The man shook his head. "It's Headman Sarath's daughter. She's friends with the boy. Her father lets her mix with all sorts." He spat on the ground.

"Get out," said General Siri to Chaya.

A guard pulled her off the path, grabbing her by the neckline of her dress, the cloth cutting into her neck. "*No*. Wait." The words stuck in her throat. Her palms slammed into gravel as he pushed her by the wayside and the sounds rolled away.

"*Please*," she screamed again. "He didn't do it. It was me." She scrabbled up and dusted her sandy, bloody hands but by then the whole convoy was disappearing into the distance.

Chaya trudged back to the workshop and sat on Neel's empty stool. She put her head down on his work table and punched the surface. Tears spilled down her face and darkened the partly carved lotuses he'd been working on.

She had to pull herself together. There was no time to waste. She was the one who'd got Neel into this and it was up to her to fix things. She looked up and dried her eyes.

There was a movement in the corner of the

workshop. Nour was standing by the far wall.

"What on earth?" Chaya glared at her.

"I'm sorry about what happened," said Nour. "I really—"

"Go away," said Chaya. "You shouldn't be here."

"You tried to take the blame." Nour seemed to consider Chaya, her head cocked to one side.

"I *am* to blame." Chaya got up and paced the room. She had to help Neel. What could she do?

"Why did you do it?" said Nour.

"Do *what*? Would you just leave? I don't have time for this right now."

But Nour stayed where she was, staring outside as if deep in thought. "I mean," she said, turning to Chaya briefly, "you know the consequences of being caught. Why did you say you did it? Even if it was true."

"Because Neel is my *friend*. Is that so hard to understand?"

Nour stared at Chaya for a few moments before turning back to the outside again.

Chaya picked up Neel's carving tools that had been scattered on the floor when he was dragged out. She felt Nour's eyes on her as she wrapped them in a rag and dropped them into her pocket.

"Where are you going?" asked Nour as Chaya made

for the outside.

Chaya ignored her.

"Wait." Nour hurried up behind. "Aren't you going to help your friend?"

Chaya turned to her sharply. "Of course I am."

"How?" Nour ran beside Chaya, struggling to keep up on the narrow path without stumbling into the paddy field. "How will you help him?"

"By doing what I do best."

"And what's that?"

"Breaking into places and making off with stuff," said Chaya, and strode away as Nour stared after her in surprise.

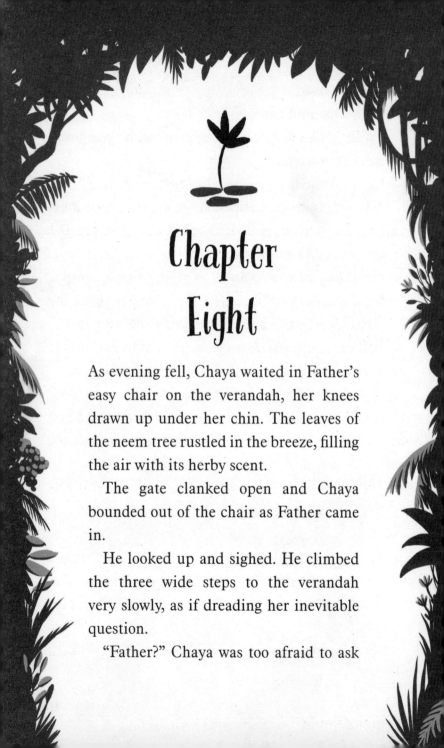

Chapter Eight

As evening fell, Chaya waited in Father's easy chair on the verandah, her knees drawn up under her chin. The leaves of the neem tree rustled in the breeze, filling the air with its herby scent.

The gate clanked open and Chaya bounded out of the chair as Father came in.

He looked up and sighed. He climbed the three wide steps to the verandah very slowly, as if dreading her inevitable question.

"Father?" Chaya was too afraid to ask

him. She could guess the answer already. The King wasn't known for his mercy.

Father sank into the easy chair but didn't lean back. He patted the chair next to him. "Come here."

"Is it bad news?" she said, taking the seat.

"Why didn't you tell me, Chaya?" He pressed his fingertips to his forehead. "Neelan, the jewel thief? I can't believe it. You must have known?"

Chaya pushed her fingers into the weaving of her seat. "He's not a thief. He really isn't, please trust me on this. There's been a mistake."

Father shook his head. "There was no mistake. He was caught with the jewels."

Could she tell him? No, Father would never turn her in – he'd lock her up at home to protect her and would never let her rescue Neel. He might even turn himself in to do the right thing by Neel.

"But a guard near the Queen's quarters said it was a girl," she said.

"That's what he insists but that can't be true, of course. He's afraid and making up things. Everyone else reported different descriptions of the boy. The truth is, people were panicking and running and no one knew who was chasing whom."

The edges of the weaving cut into her skin as Chaya

gripped it harder. "But if they just asked that guard—"

"He's been fired, Chaya."

Only one person at the palace knew that Neel wasn't the jewel thief, and he was gone.

"How could they do that?" she yelled. "He didn't do anything!"

"The King doesn't take too kindly to a breach like that. You know how it is. All his reign he's been fearful of an uprising against him. With good reason."

Chaya took a deep breath and tried to calm her racing heart. "What happens now? What about Neel?"

Father took her hand. "I'm so sorry, my child. The King has given his verdict."

"No!" Chaya got up and snatched her hand away. "No. There hasn't been a trial. What about witnesses? Someone else could have planted the jewels in the workshop. That's just not fair."

"Chaya." There were tears in Father's eyes. "I know that this is hard for you. Neelan is your best and oldest friend, but he's done something terrible."

"No, he hasn't! The King can't do this. What about proof? They can't sentence an innocent person to death."

"That's just it. There's no need for proof, Chaya. The boy has confessed."

Chapter Nine

Chaya curled up in her chair while Father poured her a tumbler of water from the clay pitcher. Her body felt numb. All she could think about was Neel in a dark, lonely prison, about to pay the ultimate price for a crime *she* committed.

But if she said something, it would be Father instead.

"I spoke to his family." Father handed her the water. "I told his mother I can find her a job once she's had her baby."

Chaya pictured Neel's distraught family. His lean, stooped father, his hands fragrant with the cinnamon bark he peeled all day; his round, cheery mother; his two younger brothers and sister; and the baby sibling he might never see.

NO. Chaya sat up and thumped the tumbler down. She had to put her plan into action right away.

"Father," she said. "I want to see him."

"I don't think that's a good idea, Chaya. Even if it were possible."

"Please, Father." Chaya squeezed his wrist. "I must see him. I have to say goodbye." She'd never even seen the prison. She had to know where it was and what it was like before she planned her rescue. "Just five minutes. I want to say goodbye to him one last time."

"Chaya…" Father shook his head.

"Please, Father, please. I'll never ask you anything again. My best friend is going to *die*."

"Oh, Chaya." Father sighed. "I'll see what I can do."

Chaya clutched the paper bag of *jambu* fruits in her hand as she accompanied her father to the palace. A guard at the main entrance put his hands together in greeting to Father, and waved them through with a smile.

"It wasn't easy to make this happen," Father said as they walked up the terraced gardens. "It'll be a quick visit. You can see him, and then we'll leave." He kept looking at her from time to time. "I'm not sure if this is good for you. Seeing him now."

"We've been over this, Father," said Chaya. Her eyes swept the place. So far they'd passed through three sets of guarding posts, and they were still outdoors. "You know me. I'm not going to beat my chest and wail. I just need to see him one last time."

Father pursed his lips. He took a pathway that ran in the opposite direction to the lion's entrance.

Chaya didn't even know about this place, that the palace complex had an underground prison at the bottom, hidden from view, where the King's prisoners were held. So it wasn't just gardens and pools on the ground level. A silvery path sloped through a brick archway flecked with moss, and downwards to what looked like an underground complex.

More guards. This time they stopped Father, examining the document giving them access. One looked quizzically at Chaya, but Father quickly pointed out the clause authorising her on the document too, and he waved them through.

Wide stone steps dipped down into a dark building. Even the stairs had guards on either end. This was going to be tough. Chaya bit into one of the *jambu* fruits from her bag, savouring its sweetness.

"Come on," said Father, taking her arm. "Have you changed your mind? We could just go home."

"No," said Chaya. "I was just looking. I didn't know about this place."

"It's not very pleasant," said Father. "But we won't be staying long."

She crunched another *jambu* while going down the stairs. All the guards appeared to be looking straight ahead but she could feel their eyes following her and Father as they passed.

The building was dark after the brightness outside, and smelled of sweat and damp rags. A guard at the doorway checked the document again. He called out to a scrawny young man. "Take them to the jewel thief."

Chaya bristled at that. Neel had a name. She glared at the guard as she crunched her *jambu* and followed the young man inside.

He unlocked a large iron-grille door, and it clanged open. A bare corridor lay ahead, tiny windows set in the walls on one side. On the other side were the cells. As they walked down Chaya looked straight in front. It seemed wrong to look at the prisoners, as if they were on display. Even so she could sense them staring at her through iron bars. Right at the end the guard unlocked a cell gate and pushed it open. "Go on," he said.

Neel was sitting on the floor of the tiny cell. He looked red-eyed and worn, but got up and greeted Father with his palms together as soon as he saw them. He smiled at Chaya, his pastel-blue shirt now brown, and a gash running across one cheek. A stab of anger sliced through Chaya.

"Neelan." Father's voice was gentle. "How are you doing, boy?"

Neel nodded. "Thank you for coming. Nice to see you too, Chaya." He sounded like he had a bad cold.

"Hi, Neel," she said. Her eyes swept over the cell. It was only about six feet by six, no windows, but there was one directly outside the bars in the corridor.

"Are those for me?" Neel was pointing to the bag in her hand.

"Oh, yes," she said, pushing the *jambu* at him. The window was too small for her. Wasn't it? She squinted at it.

"Thanks," he said, looking into the bag. "Even though you've eaten most of them."

"What?" Chaya frowned. "Oh. Sorry, I was distracted." She shook her head. "There's still loads *at the bottom.*" She gave him a meaningful look, but he seemed bewildered.

Father patted Neel. "Has your family been again, Neelan?"

"No, sir. They were allowed yesterday, but not any more."

"That's not right. I'll see what I can do, OK?" Father looked at Neel kindly, but seemed unsure about what to say. "They must want to be with you at this time."

"It's all right, sir. It's better this way."

The guards were everywhere. How on earth would she get in here to get Neel out?

"But about my family, sir," said Neel. "Without my wages…"

"I understand, Neelan," said Father. "Don't worry about that at all. They will be taken care of, I'll make sure of that. I couldn't help you, boy," Father's voice broke slightly, "but I won't let your family down."

There was only one entrance into the hall with the cells. And the windows… Even if she could get in, could Neel get out through one?

"Thank you, sir. That means a lot."

Chaya gripped the cold iron bars of the cell. She had about twenty hours till Neel was taken away to his death.

"I wish I could do more. For you." Father cleared his throat, and looked at Chaya. "Right. We'd better go before they come and ask us to. I'll be here tomorrow, Neelan."

"Bye, Neel." Chaya strode out ahead of Father. What was at the back of the cell block anyway? It would be useful to know what was beyond the wall of Neel's cell. Maybe if they wandered that way she might find out.

But when they got to the area outside the cell block the young man was waiting for them. Without a word he ushered them out the same way they came in.

"What was all that about?" Father stared at Chaya.

"What?" Chaya squinted up at the canopy of trees. Sometimes trees were useful. People never looked upwards.

"After all that, you hardly said a word to Neelan! What was all that looking around everywhere except at him?"

Chaya shrugged. "People grieve in different ways." She watched Father's face to see if he had any clue what she was planning, but he seemed quite sure it was over for Neel.

Father squeezed her hand. "I am so sorry about all this. For you. Neel. His family."

She squeezed his hand back. If only she could tell him she had no intention of letting Neel go to his death.

His tools, which she'd hidden at the bottom of the bag of *jambu* fruits, would be useful to him, but she wasn't counting on just that.

No, this job was mostly Chaya's.

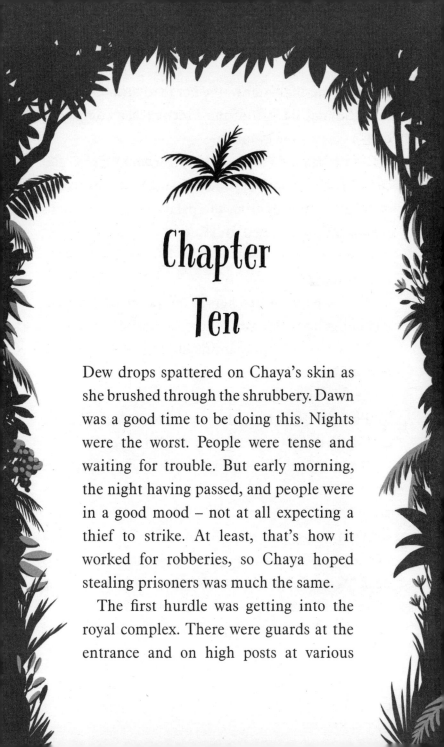

Chapter Ten

Dew drops spattered on Chaya's skin as she brushed through the shrubbery. Dawn was a good time to be doing this. Nights were the worst. People were tense and waiting for trouble. But early morning, the night having passed, and people were in a good mood – not at all expecting a thief to strike. At least, that's how it worked for robberies, so Chaya hoped stealing prisoners was much the same.

The first hurdle was getting into the royal complex. There were guards at the entrance and on high posts at various points along the outer walls, not to mention the ones dotted along the top of the inner palace compound with a view of the grounds.

Chaya leaned against an ironwood tree and considered her options. She was safe here, this patch of wilderness away from the palace where she could see without being seen. But how to proceed?

There was a rustling behind her, and a red-clad figure emerged.

"*You!*" Chaya pushed herself off the tree. "What are you doing here? Are you following me?"

"N-no," said Nour, panting slightly and adjusting her head covering. "I was … going for a walk."

"At this time of the morning? A likely story."

"I heard your friend, the boy…" Nour looked down and scuffed the ground with a beaded shoe.

Chaya sighed. "I don't know what you expect me to say. Thank you for your interest. Now, please go away."

"That thing you said the other day?" said Nour, looking up. Chaya was beginning to wonder if she was deaf. "What did you mean when you said you're going to break in somewhere and steal something?"

"Listen, I'm touched by your concern. But I'm kind of busy at the moment. I don't have time to chat, OK?"

Nour looked from Chaya to the palace complex in the distance, the lion statue pale and faded as it rose up against the dawn mist. "Are you going to rescue the boy?"

"*Will you—*"

"I can help you."

"You?" Chaya had a sudden urge to laugh.

"I figured out how to open the box, didn't I?"

Chaya ignored that. "*You*, the daughter of Cassim the merchant, who wears silk dresses and fancy shoes as everyday clothes. Who can be spotted a mile off in your sequinned finery?"

Nour scowled. "What's wrong with that?"

The girl obviously lived on another planet.

"Nothing," said Chaya. "There's nothing wrong with it. Just leave me alone." She darted away and sped off into the wilderness adjoining the east side of the royal complex. There was no point engaging with Nour. She'd done enough damage already.

Chaya took the long way round, ducking behind the palace and emerging on the other side. This was the western end of the complex, next to the temple where she had her lessons on a Wednesday. The temple's white pinnacle towered up, piercing the now milky early morning sky.

There it was. *The temple*. Her gateway into the palace, and Neel.

The temple even shared a wall with the palace. On Sundays and full-moon days the monks went into the Queen's prayer hall through a pathway connecting the two. And from there, it would be just a matter of Chaya sneaking into the underground prison.

All she needed was to get into the temple. That was the first hurdle.

Chaya hesitated by the low boundary wall. Why would she be going in today, a Thursday, when she had no lessons? What if one of the monks asked her? Her teacher, the old monk Mahanama, might be there for all she knew.

She turned away and squinted into the empty road. A red shape was moving slowly ahead, towards the city gates.

Chaya sighed. There was no other way. Nour was her ticket into the temple.

She hurried up the road, running along the length of dazzling-white scalloped walls. "Hey," she called out.

Nour turned around, a startled look on her face.

"You said you wanted to help." Chaya slowed down as she reached Nour.

Nour eyed her suspiciously. "I did."

"Well, come with me to the temple."

"To pray for the boy? You do know I pray to a different god?"

"No, not to pray. To rescue him."

Nour cocked her head. "Why go to the temple then?"

"You'll see. Come on."

Chapter Eleven

Chaya hurried back down the road, checking to see if Nour was following. They passed the usually bustling entry into the city, the pale morning glow bouncing off the white brickwork as their footsteps echoed in the deserted road. Nour caught up with Chaya and walked beside her, silent but pink-faced with excitement.

Chaya stopped at the entrance to the temple. The sparkling-white dome towered mountainous in front of them. At the foot of it a line of child monks in their saffron-coloured robes walked to their morning lessons. A quiver of excitement was beginning to tingle in Chaya as they went into the compound.

"OK, so this is what I want you to do," she said. "I'm going to show you around."

Nour frowned. "Why?"

They followed the path, Nour staring at the heart-shaped leaves of the peepul tree on the side.

"Well, I'm not really. That's what I'm pretending to do. You're a foreigner, you want to see things. I need an excuse to be here."

"Do you study here or something?"

A monk nodded at Chaya and Nour as he swept leaves off the grounds, the *ekels* of his broom rasping on the stonework.

Chaya put her palms together in greeting and smiled at him as they passed. "Yes, but I don't have lessons today," she said to Nour. "Anyway, don't ask questions. Leave your shoes here."

Nour looked like she was about to protest, but complied. Her heavily beaded shoes looked out of place beside the few straggly sandals already there.

Chaya looked around the compound as she tugged off her shoes. No one was within earshot. The monk in the compound stamped the broom on the ground and went round to the back. "So I go in with you. If anyone asks, you know why we're here. Me, I'm going to sort of disappear."

They stepped into the temple. It was dark inside, the stone floor cold under their feet and the smell of coconut oil in the tiny clay lamps lingering in the air.

"What does 'sort of disappear' even mean?" said Nour. "Either you disappear or you don't."

"Fine, I'm going to disappear."

"Where to?"

"That," said Chaya, making for an arched passage, "is none of your business."

"In *that* case," Nour started back towards the entrance, "you're on your own."

"Hey!" Chaya ran up behind Nour, her voice echoing through the passage. "What's wrong with you? You said you wanted to help."

"I do. But you want to do everything your own way."

Chaya was confused. "So?"

"So you can't expect people to help if you don't tell them things."

"Why not? Once I disappear, your part's over." Chaya made a slashing action with her hand to emphasise the *over.* "I only need you as a reason to *be* in the temple. Once I'm gone, you can leave."

"Leave?"

"Yeah. Go home. Go for a walk. Eat those sugary sweets on your sideboard. Whatever."

Nour scowled. "I'm not going to—"

"Chaya?" Soft footsteps padded down the curving passage and her teacher Mahanama shuffled into view. "Is that you, dear?"

Chaya glared at Nour. This would never have happened if Nour had just done as she was told and not argued. "Yes, Master."

"What are you doing here so early? It's not Friday, is it?" He peered at Nour, readjusting his robe over one stooping shoulder. "Who is your friend?"

Chaya shuddered at *friend*. "This is Nour, Master. Her father is the merchant, Cassim. I've brought her to see our temple."

Nour smiled at him awkwardly. She didn't bow to Mahanama, but he didn't look offended.

"Ah, so you come from the land of deserts. Welcome, Nour. You are free to look around any time. I will ask Gnana to unlock the shrine room for you as well."

"That'd be excellent, Master," said Chaya. This was going better than she could have hoped. The shrine room was right by the passageway to the palace!

"Thank you," said Nour. "I've never seen a temple

before. Where I come from, we have mosques. They're very different."

Mahanama inclined his head. "I have seen pictures. In fact, I have read many translations of books by your people. We have a few works of science and poetry here as well, brought from the great library in the north. I would love to hear more about your land, my dear. The deserts, the cities. And your journey here by sea. I think you would have many stories to tell."

Chaya nearly choked with annoyance. "It's nothing you wouldn't know already, Master."

Now it was Nour's turn to glare at her.

"I doubt that, Chaya," said Mahanama. "We all have so much to learn from each other. There's a great big world outside this island."

Nour smiled. "I'd love to come and talk to you. I could tell you about my country, and all the places I visited on the voyage here."

"Come back when you've finished looking around if you have time," said Mahanama. "And maybe, if you like, you can attend lessons here once a week like Chaya?"

"I would love that," said Nour, brightening up considerably. "But I don't know what my father would say." She seemed to droop a little at the thought.

Chaya stared at the two of them. Nour? Learn Sanskrit and the sciences at the temple like she did? Nour wasn't even in normal school, so why should she get to have these extras?

"We have to go," she snapped at Nour. "Master, I'll show her around and then we'll leave. We won't take long."

"Oh, that's all right, my dear. Take your time." Mahanama nodded at Nour, then moved off shakily using his stick. He stopped and looked at Chaya. "You're a fair person always, Chaya. Remember to also be a kind person."

"Yes, Master." As soon as Mahanama was out of sight she tugged at Nour's arm. "Come on."

Nour followed her up the passage.

"What are you playing at?" said Chaya. "You're just here as a cover. What was that whole sweet-as-jaggery act just now?"

"What *act*?" said Nour. "Some people are just naturally nice, you know."

Chaya was saved from replying by a passing monk, who smiled and nodded at her. "Early lesson today, miss?" he asked.

"No, we're just looking around," said Chaya. She wished these monks didn't start their day so early.

She'd seen so many of them already.

He was back a few moments later with a large iron key. "Master Mahanama asked me to open the shrine room for you, miss." He bustled in front, up a narrow passage to a thick, ancient-looking door.

He jiggled the key in the lock and pushed open the door with a loud grating noise. "Take your time looking around. I'll come by and lock up later."

Nour stared at the dozens of statues built along the wall.

"They're very old," Chaya said to Nour, for the benefit of the monk who was leaving. "Made in … er … a very long time ago."

Chaya went to the door and peeped out into the passage. The monk was gone. She turned back to Nour. "OK, your part ends here. Walk around a bit and then leave in fifteen minutes." She darted off towards the open door at the end of the passage that led to the temple grounds, where she could see a reposing statue nestled in the greenery outside. She stopped and turned back to Nour in the shrine room. "Thank you. You've … been a great help."

She scurried off, her bare feet slapping on the gritty stone floor. Outside, wilted frangipani flowers lay at the foot of a giant statue near the palace entryway.

Next to it was the steep flight of steps to the threshold to the palace complex. She ran nimbly up it.

"Miss Chaya?" A surprised voice rang out.

She whipped round at the top of the stairs.

It was the temple keeper, staring up at her puzzled. "What are you doing up there? Are you trying to get into the *palace*?"

Chapter Twelve

Chaya looked around and touched her chest. "Who, me?"

The temple keeper frowned. "Yes, you. Who else?"

"I, er…" He was staring at her now, and it wasn't a very friendly stare. She tried to think of an excuse. "Are we not allowed to be up here then?"

"No, and I'm sure you know that." He came up the steps towards her slowly. "And who are *we*?"

"It's my friend, Nour. I was just showing her around the temple."

"And? Where is she?"

"She…" Chaya gulped. An idea struck her. "That's what I'm wondering! I've been searching all over for her."

The keeper stopped and laughed. "Couldn't you have told me that, silly girl? Here I was wondering if you were up to some mischief."

"What, me?" Chaya laughed, trying not to overdo it. "Never."

"Well, I've got to go back to my tasks. If I see your little friend wandering about I'll tell her you were looking for her."

"Thanks." Chaya watched him go back into the passage leading to the shrine room.

She peeped out from the gateway into the green lawns and rectangular pools of the royal complex. A tiny walkway snaked in front of her, heading through the palace grounds and upwards into the Queen's prayer hall.

Chaya looked around and took a deep breath. In about six hours Neel would be taken out of his underground prison cell, on the way to his death.

She patted her pocket to check she still had the explosives. She was ready. Chaya stepped over the threshold and into the walkway.

She was inside the royal complex.

Chaya strode purposefully down the walkway. If someone were to see her now, no excuse would save her. She left the path and went into the terraced gardens, creeping downwards from the side.

She crouched behind a low wall and took stock of her surroundings. This was the ground level, with the wide promenade in front of her. In the distance she could just about make out two guards on either side of the bricked archway into the prison complex.

Chaya edged towards it, keeping close to the palace's boundary wall. The good thing was there was plenty of greenery on the prison side. Unlike the manicured lawns and delicate foliage of the formal gardens, the entry to the prison compound was full of mighty trees and rough shrubbery.

She froze as one of the patrolling figures turned towards her. She stayed stock-still, hoping she blended into the surroundings in her dirt-coloured clothes. The figure turned back as it continued to pace around the grounds.

Chaya continued on, almost flat against the boundary. High guard posts stood at regular intervals along the wall, but luckily for her they were looking *outside* at intruders trying to get in. She passed low under them, so close she could hear snatches of conversations inside each of them.

"Going to the wrestling with Samar this weekend?" said one of the guards to another, as Chaya passed stealthily under them.

"Leela is getting popular. I don't think the big boss will be happy," laughed someone in the next guard post.

"Urgh, dinner at my grandma's again. Her yam pudding's so runny," went the chat in the next post, and so on, the guards going on with their inane chatter as Chaya crept ever closer towards Neel.

At last Chaya was on the prison side. She climbed deftly up a *hal* tree, her toes gripping its gnarled bark. At the top she moved over from branch to branch, avoiding an annoyed monkey and getting as close as possible to the prison entrance on its overhead canopy of trees.

She froze at the sound of a voice below.

"He's pretty young, isn't he?"

Chaya leaned over and peered down through the leaves. Two guards sat on a boulder, munching on sticks of sugar cane.

"I mean, he was actually crying at one point. It's not right."

Chaya felt a stab of pain right through her heart.

"Shh," said the other. "Someone might hear. We can't question these things."

"Yeah, I better keep my mouth shut. I just feel … shame."

The guards fell silent, as only the crunch-crunching of their sugar cane broke through the rustle of the trees.

Chaya moved to the end of the branch, and swung on to a wood-apple tree next to it. The branch dipped down dangerously under her weight, and she scrabbled to grab something firm. A wood-apple fell from an upper branch and bounced down near her. Chaya lunged for it, rocking the branch again, and a few more of the hard fruits fell down below.

Down to where the guards were sitting.

Chaya held her breath.

"Ow," said a guard, rubbing his head where the fruit had struck. He swore and lobbed the fruit hard against a tree, where it cracked on the trunk and fell down, the brown pulp rolling away.

Chaya held her breath. As long as they didn't look

up, she was fine.

"What was that?" said the other guard.

And he looked up.

Chapter Thirteen

Chaya froze, crouching low on the branch, her hands gripping the stalks growing out of either side.

The man stared up in her direction, then shook his head. "Stupid monkeys are a menace," he said to his partner.

Chaya exhaled. Hopefully the man was just short-sighted.

She moved along through the branches, jumping from tree to tree, sometimes coming across a group of monkeys. They stared as she passed, an intruder in their territory.

Finally she was directly over the prison building. Somewhere in there sat Neel, waiting as the hours ticked away.

Now she needed to create a diversion. She stuck her hand into her pocket and drew out a stash of fireworks. They were from the New Year celebrations. She'd found them in Father's shed, then spent some time stringing them together. And one of the good-for-nothing boys from the riverside that Aunty so despised had also helped her with a device to cause a smokescreen. But that was for later.

She struck a match and lit the end of the string. It fizzled and sparked up, the flame zipping downwards at speed. Chaya drew her arm back and threw it as hard as she could.

She knew exactly what she was aiming for. The explosives fell at the back of the prison, where the open kitchen was and where she knew nobody would be at this time of the morning. The whole thing exploded mightily, bits of clay pots and pans shooting all over the place and clumps of old congee splatting into the air.

Chaya was nearly thrown out of the tree in spite of bracing herself for the noise. Around her the trees vibrated and monkeys screeched, and from below came shouts and the sound of panicked running. A line of dish rags caught fire, and guards came pouring into the area from all over.

Chaya swung down and dashed into the prison building.

The place smelled as bad as before, all dampness and sweat, but no one was about in the entrance hall. She hurried to the passage of cells she had visited the previous day. The iron railing barred it, locked shut.

"Neel!" she shouted through the bars. "Neel, can you hear me?"

All she could see was a toothless man in the first cell, who surveyed her with interest.

An answering cry came from the last cell. "Ch-Chaya?" Neel sounded incredulous.

"Yes! Neel, where are the keys to the gate?"

There was a roar and crackle of the fire, and a gust of smoky air blew in through the entrance.

"I … I'm not sure," said Neel, and his hands gripped the iron bars at the bottom of the passage. "What are you doing here? Get out before they find you."

"I'm going to get you out first. Let me go and look for the keys."

That made two doors to unlock before freeing Neel.

"You need Jansz," said the toothless man in

the first cell.

"Pardon?" said Chaya.

The man looked at her impassively. "That's the man who's in charge of the keys."

"Do you know where he keeps them?"

But he stared through her as if he had never been talking at all.

"I take it that's a no then. OK, hold on tight, Neel. I'll be back."

The outer hall was still empty, and through the doorway over the top of the stairs she saw thick black smoke in the air. Something else seemed to have caught fire. Chaya paused for a moment and listened. Hopefully no one was hurt. There was a cacophony of shouts and water sloshing as guards fought to contain the fire.

Chaya coughed, her throat feeling itchy and dry. The keys had to be here somewhere. She hunted all around, but there was no sign of them. She bent over the ledge under which the prison logs were kept and swept her hand around the recess to check if they were there.

Heavy footsteps sounded on the stairs. Chaya sprang up on the ledge and hoisted herself on to a torch bracket on the wall. A very large man with an open mouth and chipped teeth tramped into the entrance hall, a chinking noise coming from him every time he moved. She watched him from her perch above, and when he passed under her she saw something glint at his side. The man had a bunch of keys on his belt.

A bunch of keys.

So this must be Jansz.

Chaya dropped down on top of him and grabbed for the keys. He staggered around with her on his head, roaring while she threw a canister to the ground. Smoke billowed everywhere.

Jumping off the guard, she raced to the railing and fitted a key into it. She bent low to see through the smoke, fitting key after key with shaking hands while Jansz staggered towards her through the haze.

One of the keys slotted in and Chaya yanked the gate open with a loud creak. She was slipping through when she was pulled up short by a jerk from behind as Jansz lifted her clean off the floor.

As the smoke cleared, she found herself face to face with him, pressed against the wall with her feet dangling above the ground. "Really sorry," she said. "I shouldn't have done that."

Jansz's nostrils flared as he brought his face, purple with rage, closer to Chaya's.

Chapter Fourteen

Jansz slammed Chaya against the wall, a sharp pain slicing through her head as it hit the stone. His hands closed around her neck.

"Hey, wai—" Chaya's words were cut off as his hands tightened round her throat.

She kicked and clawed at the man but his grip only increased. She had to do something or she was going to be of no use to Neel.

The world edged into black.

Then Chaya slammed on to the ground

where she was roughly shaken. A dark face swam into view.

What was happening? Had Jansz changed his mind? Chaya blinked, and someone yanked her to her feet.

"Chaya, focus. We need to get out."

It wasn't Jansz.

"Neel?"

Neel's blurry face hovered in front of her.

Chaya swallowed down nausea as the view slowly solidified. Jansz lay on the floor, blocking the whole passage.

"Don't worry," said Neel. "He's coming to already."

Chaya shook her groggy head. "Neel, how on earth?"

"The tools you brought me, Chaya. I was sawing all last night. Managed to get out just in time."

Chaya whooped. Things were on track again. The bunch of keys were on the floor and she kicked them under the bars to the toothless man in the first cell. "There you go. A gift from us. Let's go, Neel."

They darted out into the hall and started up the steps.

And that was when they saw them. Every one – and it did look like every single one – of the guards had returned and they were all staring at Chaya and Neel with undisguised anger.

Chaya felt pressed in on all sides as the guards surrounded her and Neel. She was swept up in the throng, and half dragged, half carried up the stairs and out of the underground prison. On the edge of her vision Neel was being borne away too.

She blinked in the sudden daylight. "Where are you taking us?"

"Straight to General Siri. Let's see you try to get out of this," said a man. "You and your friend can both lose your heads."

On the promenade more guards joined the dozens already surrounding the children, pushing them towards the palace.

There was a shout from somewhere above, and Chaya felt a shock ripple through the swarm of guards.

"Hey!" came a familiar voice. A figure stood high up on the steps leading to the inner palace, silhouetted against the giant lion statue.

A figure in a floaty red dress.

"Hey, fools! Look behind you," yelled Nour.

The throng turned round, and the guards went crazy. There were shouts of dismay as they shot off back the way they'd come. Chaya stood on tiptoe to try to see over the people. Whatever was going on?

All the prisoners had escaped and were currently making their way to freedom. The toothless man from the first cell was at the front, running away merrily.

Chaya slipped out of her guard's grasp while he was distracted. He tried to grab her by the plait but she twisted away from him and ran. Someone stuck out his foot and sent her flying till she landed with a thwack on the gravelled ground, hands outstretched. Another guard brought his foot down over her hand, but she whipped it away just in time and bounded up, sprinting between two other men coming her way. She could see Neel up ahead, also free and running. He slowed down to let her catch up.

"No – go, Neel," shouted Chaya. "Meet you at the *jambu* tree."

Neel sped off. A young guard pulled at her but she kicked him away. Two of the King's men were heading for her. Chaya changed direction, zigzagging through the formal gardens. One of them was gaining on her. He ran up and caught the edge of her skirt. She plucked it away and turned a corner. A small flight of steps led downwards.

Chaya missed her footing and slipped.

And went crashing down the steps.

She landed in a heap at the bottom. Pain shot

through her ankle and she screamed. She bit down on her fist and crawled into a bush of coral flames.

"She's here somewhere. She's got to be." There was a sound of thrashing leaves as the men searched through the foliage.

Chaya inched her way through the shrubbery. She circled her ankle with her hand and the warmth soothed the pain a little. She couldn't put her weight on it – she'd just have to crawl. How on earth would she get to Neel at the *jambu* tree?

There was a shout of triumph. "Look, she's dropped something."

"A box of matches! It *was* her then. Wait till I get her to General Siri."

Chaya dragged herself towards the walled garden. It was at the back of the palace complex and removed from all the action, so quiet and still. She had to bite painfully on her lip to keep herself from crying out every time she moved.

It was finished. *She* was finished. Even if by some miracle she got out of the royal palace safely, she couldn't possibly get to the *jambu* tree where Neel was waiting.

But at least he wasn't in immediate danger any more. And Father would be safe too. Even if she was caught, nothing would be traced back to him. Father had no vested interest in releasing Neel.

Even if he lost his job, at least he wouldn't lose his life.

Dizziness threatened to overcome her. Chaya squeezed her eyes shut and tried to block out the pain. They would find her. It was over.

No.

Her eyes flew open. She was no quitter. Chaya hauled herself into the walled garden. The green was quiet, with no one in sight. The servants must have left their positions and gone to the front of the complex, drawn by all the chaos.

Chaya stood up and ran. A searing pain shot through her leg all the way up. It was useless. She was in too much pain. This was it; they'd find her here eventually.

And then in the distance, through a blur of pain, Chaya saw her getaway vehicle. She hobbled up and untied the chain from the post. Black spots swam in front of her eyes as she scrambled up and felt the calming, gentle sway take her off to find Neel.

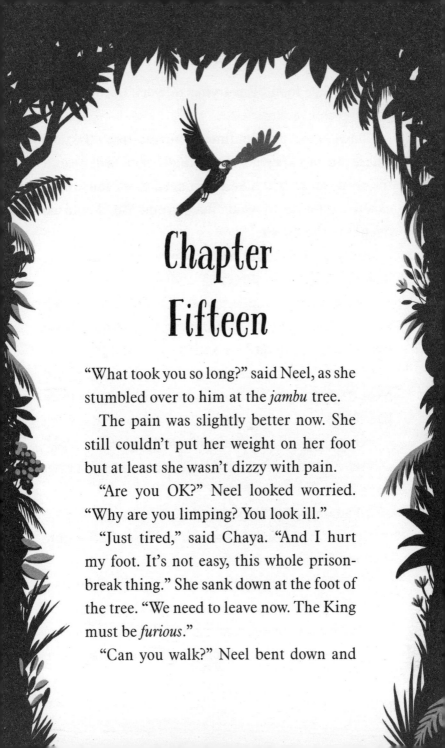

Chapter Fifteen

"What took you so long?" said Neel, as she stumbled over to him at the *jambu* tree.

The pain was slightly better now. She still couldn't put her weight on her foot but at least she wasn't dizzy with pain.

"Are you OK?" Neel looked worried. "Why are you limping? You look ill."

"Just tired," said Chaya. "And I hurt my foot. It's not easy, this whole prison-break thing." She sank down at the foot of the tree. "We need to leave now. The King must be *furious*."

"Can you walk?" Neel bent down and

stared at her foot. "I'm trying to work out where to go."

Chaya stood up, holding on to the tree. "I know where we *shouldn't* go. The King's men will search the road out of the village. We need to do something exactly opposite to what they expect. We should go deep into the jungle."

"Are you mad?" said Neel. "We're just going to get lost."

"We have no other choice." Chaya took a step forward and winced. "It'll buy us some time till we figure out what to do."

"You can't go anywhere by the looks of it," said Neel. "Chaya, you've done enough. I'll take it from here."

"Neel, they saw me. *Again.* It's too late for that now."

Neel rubbed his head. "What a mess. You can't even walk. How did you get here?"

"I had, er, some help. Anyway, I do have a way we can go into the jungle. Sprained ankle and all. Come with me."

Chaya led the way, keeping well into the wilderness. She let her foot drag along, careful not to put any weight on it. Neel didn't say much. He looked worried and tired. After all the excitement of the big rescue it was funny that all they felt now was tired and subdued.

"Why couldn't you bring the cart with you?" asked Neel.

"It's not a cart, come on. Just here. Through the trees."

There was a scuffling behind them and Neel started. He clutched Chaya and began to drag her with him. "Come on, come on."

Another stab of pain went through her leg as Chaya tried to hurry.

"Hey, what are you two doing?" came a voice from behind. "Wait for me."

Chaya wheeled around, yelping with pain as the weight fell on her injured ankle.

Nour was lumbering towards them, laden with two small sacks.

"I got supplies," she said, puffing and panting. She dropped the two bags on the ground near them, one of them falling with a metallic thud.

"*Are you out of your mind?*" yelled Chaya. "What are you doing here?"

Nour stopped and screwed up her face. "You're welcome. Some gratitude wouldn't go amiss, you know."

"Miss Nour?" Neel looked horrified. "What are you doing here? How did you even know where we were?"

"I followed you, of course. Then quickly nipped back for supplies from home. I guess your friend here," she turned to Chaya, "hasn't told you that I helped rescue you, Neelan."

"Helped? I just asked you to come with me to the temple – and thank you very much for that. But that's it. Now, go home and get on with your life."

A bang sounded in the distance, and they could hear galloping coming from the city.

"We need to go," said Chaya. "Come on, Neel."

She ran towards the jungle with Neel, trying not to scream with the pain. Nour followed them with her bags. "Come on, it's just here."

She found the place and stopped at the clearing. And there it was. Her rather unusual getaway vehicle.

Neel turned to her in shock. "Oh my lord, Chaya. What on earth have you done?"

"I didn't have much of a choice, you know! I was in pain and blacking out, and had to get out of there without the use of my foot!"

Nour shrieked. "What the— What kind of a kleptomaniac *are* you?"

"Shut up! I *just said* I had to steal him to get away.

Get on, Neel, we need to go *now*."

But her friend was staring in horror at the gentle bulk of Ananda, the King's own elephant.

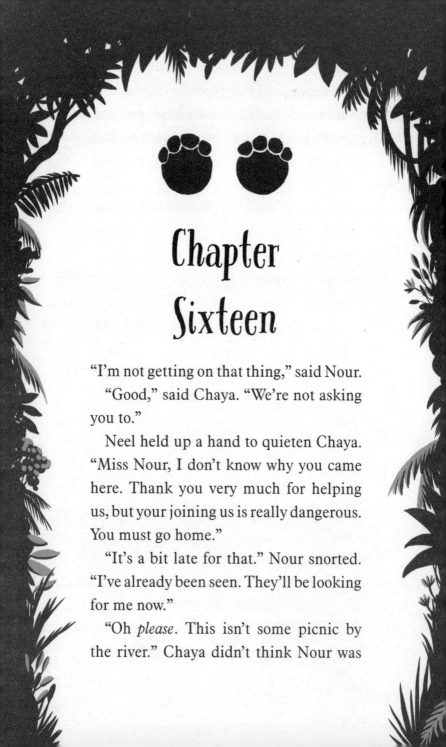

Chapter Sixteen

"I'm not getting on that thing," said Nour.

"Good," said Chaya. "We're not asking you to."

Neel held up a hand to quieten Chaya. "Miss Nour, I don't know why you came here. Thank you very much for helping us, but your joining us is really dangerous. You must go home."

"It's a bit late for that." Nour snorted. "I've already been seen. They'll be looking for me now."

"Oh *please*. This isn't some picnic by the river." Chaya didn't think Nour was taking this seriously. They were in so much danger, she didn't want an innocent like Nour, however idiotic, to be dragged in. She went to Ananda, approaching him from his right side, and stroked his grainy hide. "Er, Neel, can I talk to you for a minute?"

Nour glared at Chaya and walked away a little. She dumped the two bags on the ground and turned her back.

"We're *not* taking her," Chaya whispered when Neel came to her. "No way."

"You heard what she said," hissed Neel. "She can't go back now."

"But she can't come with us! It's out of the question."

"Why not?"

"Because…" Chaya cast around in her mind for a good enough reason. "Because, well, because she's a meat eater."

Neel frowned. "So?"

"*So?* What if she gets hungry? She might take a bite of Ananda."

"Oh, don't be ridiculous."

"Fine, but it's all on your head then." Chaya patted Ananda's back leg and commanded him to kneel, just like she'd seen the mahouts do.

"He might not respond to you," said Neel.

"Sure he will. He's very friendly. I see the palace elephants having their bath in the river all the time. I know Ananda's mahout too." She'd only spoken to him once, but whatever.

Ananda bent down and angled his leg dutifully. Chaya stood on it and hoisted herself on to his back, moving up so that she was sitting at his neck. It was good to be off her foot again. Ananda felt warm and reassuring under her.

"Miss Nour," said Neel, turning to her. "You next."

"Wait a minute." Nour looked from Neel to the elephant. "Where exactly are we going?"

"Into the jungle, Miss Nour. We'll be able to escape from the King's guards in there."

Nour's eyes widened. For the first time it looked like she realised what she'd got herself into.

Serves her right, thought Chaya.

"D-deep into that? Isn't it dangerous?"

"Well … not as much as people think," said Neel. "We have no choice really. The King's men are bound to be searching the roads out of the village right now. We have to go somewhere they wouldn't think of looking immediately."

"But is there no other option? This can't be safe for humans."

"It's not that bad, Miss Nour. Really."

"Yeah," said Chaya, from atop Ananda. "Except for the leopards."

Nour went white.

Neel glared at Chaya. "Leopards don't attack humans unless they feel threatened. As long as we keep away from them we'll be fine."

"True," said Chaya. "A leopard hasn't killed a villager in like … a whole week."

Nour whimpered under her breath.

"And the bandits," said Chaya. "Don't forget the bandits."

"Chaya! You're not helping," said Neel.

"What, are we trying to *convince* her to come with us now?"

"We've been over this," said Neel. "She can't go back."

Nour looked slightly ill.

"Miss Nour, trust me, this is the only way." Neel nodded towards the two sacks in Nour's hands. "Do you have salt in there?"

"*Salt?*" Nour looked from Neel to Chaya. "Why would I have salt?"

Chaya and Neel exchanged a glance. "It doesn't matter," said Neel. "We'll be fine."

Chaya groaned. "Look, Neel. She won't be able to stomach a journey like this."

"Oh, stop it," said Nour. "I've gone on camel journeys through the desert that last for *weeks*."

"What's a camel?" asked Neel.

Nour's mouth fell open.

"Don't you dare!" said Chaya. "Neel had to stop going to school to help his family. And who cares about a stupid camel anyway?"

Nour surveyed Ananda with something like suspicion. "How fast can this thing go?"

"This *thing* is an elephant, and he has a name. Ananda can go faster than you think."

"But how do you hide an elephant from people? It's going to be more of a problem to us than a solution."

Chaya laughed. "Ever been inside a rainforest? You're going to be so surprised, desert girl. The trees are like a canopy around you, so much so that sometimes even the sunlight can't get through."

"But won't he leave a trail? Of broken trees and stuff."

"There are *herds* of wild elephants in the jungle. It's a place of, you know, *wildlife*."

The sound of horses' hooves rent the air, much closer this time. "We need to go," said Neel. "Guess I'll be mahout then, since no one else is volunteering." He picked up a stick and went to Ananda's side. "Please get on, Miss Nour. We don't have time to lose."

Nour looked stricken and she backed away. Neel tied the two sacks together and flung the whole thing over Ananda so each sack hung either side of the elephant's back. "Come on, Miss Nour. Please get on. We need to get into the jungle."

The horses were getting closer and soon they could hear shouting.

"Miss Nour, we'll have to leave without you."

Nour scrunched up her eyes and stepped on to Ananda's bent leg. She flailed her arms at Chaya, who yanked her up on to the elephant's back. Neel hopped up nimbly behind them.

"*Go, Ananda!*" shouted Chaya, rubbing her feet on the back of Ananda's ears.

Ananda straightened his leg and rose up with a great swaying motion, making Nour scream and grab at Chaya's hair.

"Stop it!" Chaya yelled. "Don't be such a baby."

Ananda moved slowly through the wilderness, picking his way to the forest. Behind Chaya, Nour squealed and rocked as if she was on a boat, and grabbed on to the elephant's hide. Chaya wasn't sure if Nour was scared or happy, but she was making a lot of strange noises.

"Will you shut up?" she yelled over her shoulder.

Ananda lurched towards the jungle, gradually speeding up. He crashed through the foliage, his powerful tusks smashing their way between gaps. Chaya ducked as branches scratched and tugged at them. With the jungle appearing just ahead, Neel tapped Ananda gently on the side and urged him on. Ananda gathered speed and barrelled his way into the undergrowth with Nour shrieking loudly as they plunged into its depths.

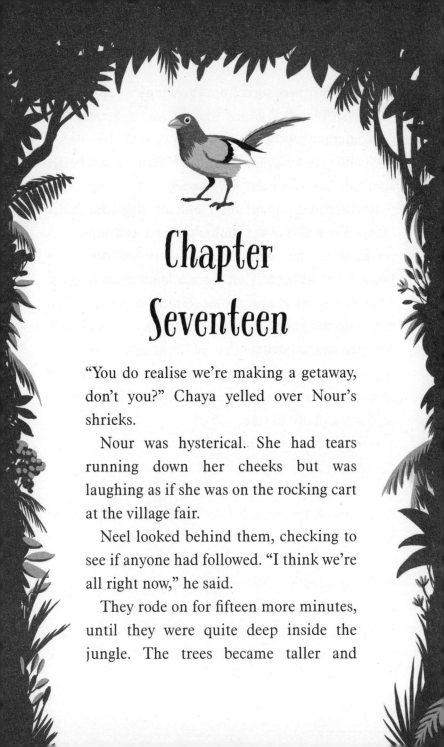

Chapter
Seventeen

"You do realise we're making a getaway, don't you?" Chaya yelled over Nour's shrieks.

Nour was hysterical. She had tears running down her cheeks but was laughing as if she was on the rocking cart at the village fair.

Neel looked behind them, checking to see if anyone had followed. "I think we're all right now," he said.

They rode on for fifteen more minutes, until they were quite deep inside the jungle. The trees became taller and malkoha chirps echoed from their tops.

"Stop, Ananda," called out Chaya, squeezing her legs together gently.

Neel slid down Ananda's side. "Chaya, you'd better stay on. Miss Nour and I will walk."

He helped Nour off the elephant. She practically skipped down as if she couldn't wait to get away.

Chaya watched Neel and Nour's heads bob beside her as they walked. They kept a leisurely pace now. The air was thick with the smell of lush greenery and damp earth. The forest was getting denser, although Ananda made short work of knocking down any obstructing foliage in the way. One foot crunched through a rotting log on the ground as easily as an axe through a plantain tree.

"OK, we need a plan," said Chaya.

"Yes, we're as safe as we can be for the moment," said Neel. "But once the King's men realise that we're not on the High Road they'll start to search the jungle."

"I have an idea." Chaya rubbed Ananda behind his right ear with her foot, steering him gently round to the left of a fallen tree. "If we keep heading south we could get to Galle. It's far enough for us to be safe from the King's men, and we can hide there till we work out how to fix things. That's where Vijay and his family are now."

"That's this boy who got attacked by a crocodile," said Neel, for the benefit of Nour. "He's being treated by a medicine man there."

"And hopefully getting better," said Chaya. "We can trust Vijay's people to take a message to our families, so we could let them know we're safe."

Neel nodded. "That makes sense. I know Galle. I've been with Master; he does a lot of trade there. There are plenty of tiny fishing villages nearby we could go to, where nobody would have heard of any of this."

"Great. All we have to do is get there without being caught. And then figure out what to do."

Chaya sneaked a glance at Nour. She hadn't the faintest idea what they were going to do about her.

They kept to the sparser parts of the jungle, well away from the thick undergrowth. After an hour of walking Chaya's stomach was growling.

The sun was high in the sky when they stopped to rest.

"I'm starving," said Chaya, sliding off Ananda. She gently put her weight on her foot to test it, and it felt only slightly tender.

"I have some food in the bag," said Nour, seating

herself on a fallen tree trunk, as far away from Ananda as possible.

Neel fetched one of the bags. Inside were two combs of ripe plantains and a bag of flatbread, and the fried sweets from the sideboard in Nour's house. Chaya took a handful of the sweets and stuffed them in her mouth. They were sugared and crunchy, and she ate ravenously. She noticed Neel do the same, although he threw one of the combs of plantains to Ananda first.

"Mmm," said Chaya. "I've been dying to taste these ever since I saw them on your sideboard the other day."

Nour looked up from picking at her food in astonishment. "You didn't take any?"

Chaya laughed. Nour didn't know her at all. "No. I didn't."

There was a sound of gentle rustling and Chaya turned to find Ananda picking leaves from high above with his trunk.

"Aunty must be furious," said Chaya.

Neel looked down at the ground. "I keep thinking of my parents, too."

"That's the first thing we should do when we get to Galle safely," said Chaya. "Send word to them."

"Mine will be glad I got away, though." Neel leaned back on a large upright stone. "They must be finding it so hard without my wages. Your father promised to help them but I need to figure out how to get back to them. How we can all get back home."

"We have to find a way to undo all this. Make the King forgive us, or disregard everything that happened."

Neel said nothing to that, and Chaya didn't blame him. Just saying it out loud sounded so ridiculous.

She licked her fingers and munched on a flatbread.

"How about you, Miss Nour?" said Neel. "Your family must be so upset. They don't even have any idea what you're mixed up in."

Nour nodded and looked down at her shoe. Something unreadable – like fear or guilt – flitted across her face.

"We'll think of something," said Neel. But he didn't sound convinced at all.

Chapter Eighteen

Chaya looked at Nour, who was smoothing the beadwork on her shoe with a fingertip. She had gone quiet, and didn't eat any more.

Neel stood up, looking much better after the meal. "Come on, we need to keep moving. We'll stop again when the sun goes down."

Nour sighed but got up too. She dusted sugar from her dress and trudged after Neel.

Chaya climbed on to Ananda and they moved off. The sun beat down as the day got hotter and hotter.

"Once Chaya's foot is properly healed you can ride the elephant, OK?" Neel said to Nour.

Nour nodded towards Ananda. "I thought they could carry loads of weight."

"They can," said Neel. "With their trunks. You should see the place where the Master and I go to buy wood. Once the trees are cut down it is elephants that lift and move the logs. And they get the elephants to put them into the river to transport them downstream."

"That's remarkable," said Nour. "I didn't know you could train them to do things like that."

"Oh, they can do all sorts; they are quite intelligent. But I don't think too many people are meant to ride them. That's why Chaya and you need to take turns."

"What about you? You should have a turn, too."

"Oh, I'm used to walking long distances. I take cinnamon from my father to traders in different parts of the island when I'm not working for the Master."

"Is your father a cinnamon peeler then?"

"Yes. I used to do it too, until the Master gave me the job in his workshop."

"What's it—"

"Will you stop talking, Nour?" said Chaya. "Honestly, we're on the run here."

Nour glared up at Chaya. "We're in the middle of a jungle. Miles away from anyone."

"Still. You never know who's listening. And anyway, Neel doesn't want to talk."

"I don't mi—" began Neel.

"He's just being polite," said Chaya to Nour. "Now, keep quiet."

Nour rolled her eyes.

Ananda padded soundlessly through the jungle, his muscles moving under his rough hide.

"Do you know if we're going the right way, Neel?" Chaya asked.

"Yes, I've been watching the shadows changing," said Neel. "We're heading south."

"Is it going to be jungle all the way?" asked Nour.

"About half of it," said Chaya before Neel could answer.

"Serendib has a lot of jungle," said Nour.

Chaya huffed. "What would you rather? Horrible dry deserts?"

"I was just making *conversation*."

"No need. We're fine without it."

When evening fell they came upon a cave, set above the ground on a thick ledge of rock.

"Finally." Chaya slid off Ananda and stretched. The day was much cooler now and a chilly breeze blew through the trees.

She stepped up on to the ledge. It was smooth and even, perfect for a fire. She looked in at the mouth of the cave and found it in near darkness. "Hopefully no leopards," she said, savouring the gasp of horror from Nour. "This is a good place to stop for the night. There's the river too, for drinking and washing."

Neel hunted on the ground and picked up a rock. "Let's make a fire. That way if anything's in the cave it should come out."

While Neel struck rocks together Chaya went and found sticks and branches for the fire. She laid them for him on the rocky ledge and soon he'd got a fire roaring.

He took a torch of burning wood into the cave. "All clear," he shouted, his voice muffled and echoey. "It's a very small cave, actually. No animals."

Nour had gone to explore their surroundings and came back with some wild *jambu* in a cone she'd made out of a large leaf.

Chaya pounced on them at once. "Woo hoo, *jambu*. But this isn't enough for our meal. What else have you got there in your bags?"

There wasn't much left. They gave Ananda the remaining comb of plantains, which only left the sweets from earlier. The rest of Nour's supplies consisted of things like bedsheets and toiletries.

Chaya sighed. It was a wonder Nour didn't bring her maid.

Neel came back with a wild breadfruit, which he cut up using his carpentry knife. He sharpened the ends of some sticks and passed them to Chaya and Nour, and they stuck chunks of breadfruit on and toasted them in the fire.

"Mmm," said Chaya, popping a piece of hot breadfruit in her mouth. It was toasted and crispy on the outside, moist and pillowy inside.

"They *are* nice," said Nour, nibbling hers delicately.

Neel threw Ananda a chunk of breadfruit, which he caught neatly in his trunk and polished off in a second. Neel laughed. "It's probably like eating a peanut to him. He needs something more substantial."

As if in answer Ananda knocked down a plantain tree with his tusks. He began stripping off its foliage bit by bit, eating almost the whole tree in a short time.

"There you go then!" Chaya laughed and rested on her elbows, munching on the toasted breadfruit.

"Father must be so worried," said Nour. "I wish I

could let him know that I'm OK."

Neel stared into the fire. "I think we all wish that." He threw another branch on the flames and the fire sparked up. "What about your mother?"

"She died three years ago," said Nour.

Chaya looked up.

"I'm sorry to hear that," said Neel.

"Thank you," said Nour. "What about you, Chaya?"

"No mother either. Died when I was a baby. Father will be worried, but at least he knows the situation."

"Really?" Neel stared at her. "He knew you were breaking into jail? What was his reaction?"

"Well, I couldn't tell him to his face, could I? I left a note at home when I came to rescue you. I figured if something went wrong, he'd better know everything."

"*How* do you even explain everything that's happened in a note?" asked Nour. "What did you say?"

"I can tell you *exactly* what I said actually." Chaya sat up and cleared her throat, striking a dramatic pose. "I wrote it so many times I have it memorised.

"*Dear Father. It wasn't Neel. I am the jewel thief. I stole the jewels during the feast at the palace, when I broke into the Queen's quarters and took them from a table by her bed. I wanted to help Vijay's family pay the medicine man for treating his leg. If I admitted to it I knew the King would never believe that I acted alone, and you'd be in danger because of me. And then Neel got arrested right in front of me. But today I'm going to rescue him. If something happens and I'm caught, I think you should know what happened and why. Please don't be disappointed in me. Your loving daughter, Chaya.*

"*P.S. This isn't really important in the grand scheme of things, but I skipped school the last two days.*"

Nour gasped, and fell about laughing when Chaya delivered the final line. Even Neel chuckled and shook his head. "You really are something else, Chaya."

"So you were telling the truth. Neelan had nothing to do with it," said Nour. "Have you done this before, Chaya?"

Chaya nodded. "Quite a few times, for different things. Someone in our village had his house destroyed in the monsoons and no one could help him. My old teacher from school got ill and lost her eyesight, so had to give up work. Then she had nothing to live on. Also one of the farmers was accidentally killed by a wild elephant that destroyed his crops. His widow needs help with money sometimes. It's for things like that."

"Who do you steal from? And what sort of things?"

"Rich people from the city, of course. That's the advantage of living so close to it. Small things like ivory ornaments and silver betel trays. I doubt they even notice they're gone." She tossed a breadfruit piece into her mouth.

Neel sighed. "No need to brag, Chaya. Look where all this has got us."

"Still," said Nour. "It all sounds rather good fun."

Chaya sputtered over her breadfruit, almost choking on it. Really, Nour was the most surprising person.

Neel groaned. "Trust me, Miss Nour. This episode has been anything but fun."

"Do you ever regret the stealing?" asked Nour, after a pause. "Even though it's from the rich."

Chaya chewed her food slowly. She noticed Neel waiting keenly for her answer. "Sometimes. Yes."

"Is your family not rich then? Your father is the headman of Nirissa."

"Of course not. A headman's just a representative from the village. Every village has one. If there's an issue the headman takes it to the palace on the people's behalf. That kind of thing. He gets a small wage and certain privileges, that's all."

"Tell me about stealing the Queen's jewels." Nour

leaned forward, her expression eager in the glow of the fire. "What made you take them?"

Chaya shrugged. "It's not like the royals have ever earned any of their wealth. When I saw that blue sapphire my hands automatically grabbed the lot. Blue is my favourite colour, and there wasn't a lot of time for thinking."

Nour looked impressed. "Weren't you afraid of getting caught?"

"Not really. Not a *lot* at that point. Who needs so much stuff anyway? It made me mad rather than afraid."

Nour pondered this for a while. "Do you think the King would let you off if he knew that you stole to help his people?"

Chaya snorted. "Not a *chance*. The King is too paranoid about his position and would worry that would make him look weak. Don't forget, he banished his own half-brother as a child because he saw him as a threat."

"A threat, why?"

"The King isn't of full royal blood," said Neel, "but his half-brother, Sena, is."

Chaya nodded. "He was afraid the people would believe Sena had the greater claim to the throne."

"So where's Sena now?"

Chaya shrugged. "He was sent away twelve years ago. The young prince, his little sister and their small entourage were banished by ship. They were never heard of again."

"But what happened to them?"

"No one knows. There've been rumours for years that the prince has returned and is plotting the King's overthrow. The King probably wishes he'd killed them all instead now."

Nour gasped. "He sounds horrible. But I love these stories. Tell me about the Queen."

"I don't know if there's much to say about her. She has a nice room and too many jewels and wouldn't have missed the ones I took."

Nour laughed. Firelight danced at the mouth of the cave and everything felt safe for the moment. Chaya was even beginning to feel sleepy.

"Right, we should turn in," said Neel. "We have Ananda to guard us as we sleep."

The inside of the cave glowed dimly from the dying embers of the fire. Chaya stretched out on the cool floor, which was hard but not uncomfortable. She could hear Nour close by, her beaded dress scraping on the ground as she curled up to sleep. She tossed a sheet over to Chaya in the dark.

There was a thump from outside as Ananda settled down for the night. Chaya felt a rush of affection for him. He was her getaway vehicle first, saving her from the King's men. Then he carried her all that time through the jungle while she rested her ankle. Now he was their very own guard elephant, lying outside in the dark while they drifted off to sleep.

Chapter Nineteen

The next morning, Chaya returned to the cave cool and refreshed.

"Where have you been?" asked Neel, rubbing his eyes and yawning. He'd been sleeping outside.

"To the river, for a wash."

Neel stretched. "About time! I did that hours ago. Let's get ready and move on then. We can eat as we go. Nour," he shouted into the cave, "come on, we need to get started. River at the back for washing."

Nour emerged from the cave, crumpled

and yawning. "River? Oh no, is it deep?"

"Yeah," said Chaya. "So deep you can see your ankles when you stand in it." She gathered up Nour's bags that were lying outside from the night before.

"OK, I'll be back in a minute." Nour tore off a pleated wrapper from a cake of soap as she set off for the river. "Don't leave without me!"

Chaya went into the cave with one of the bags. "Glad you're not calling her Miss Nour any more," she said to Neel. The place was full of Nour's jasmine scent.

"That would be weird now. She's all right, you know." Neel picked up a sheet from the floor and handed it to Chaya. "She's nice."

Nice? Neel seemed to have forgotten that it was Nour who ruined everything by buying the box and taking the jewels. Chaya scrunched up Nour's sheet and rammed it into the bag. She went out of the cave into the sunshine.

"What *is* that smell by the way?" Neel sniffed the air. "It's wherever Nour goes. It's very familiar but I can't place it."

"No idea," said Chaya, tying the two sacks together and putting them on Ananda. "She must have stepped in something. Come on, we should get going."

Neel picked up his mahout stick and Chaya hoisted herself on to the kneeling elephant.

Nour appeared and they all set off together.

A few hours later Chaya swapped places with Nour. She slipped down the side of Ananda on to the rutted ground.

"Your turn," she said to Nour. "But less of the screeching, OK?"

Neel stopped and got Ananda to kneel down for Nour. She screwed up her eyes tightly and got on.

"Do you think we're going the right way?" Chaya asked Neel.

Neel looked up at the sky, and then the shadows of the trees. "I think so. It's hard to know for certain. I hope we can go in as much of a straight line as possible, aiming for the sea to the south. We should come to a mountainous area of the jungle by tomorrow if we're on the right track. If we're not, we'll be in uncharted territory."

Chaya shuddered. The denser the jungle got, the more chances of leeches crawling up them. And they didn't have any salt. If they didn't have ready access to a fire they'd just have to wait it out while the leeches sucked out their blood and fell off themselves.

"We're fine for the moment though," she said. "But I wish it wasn't so hot today."

"And I'm thirsty," said Nour. "I wish we had water."

"We should come to water soon," said Neel. "Hopefully."

But an hour later the sun had risen higher and the day grew sweltering. Chaya's clothes stuck to her back. At least her ankle was better and she wasn't in pain any more.

Nour seemed to be wilting on top of Ananda. "We should have brought water with us."

"It's no use complaining now," said Chaya. "You should have brought a bottle instead of bed sheets. Would have been more useful to us."

"Why didn't *you* bring one then, since you know everything?"

"I was too busy rescuing Neel from death."

"So what? I brought stuff. And I didn't see you complain when you were stuffing yourself with my food yesterday."

Neel rubbed the back of his hand over his head, making his sodden hair stick up like a wet crow's feathers. "Chaya, Nour, please can we—"

"Bed sheets!" shouted Chaya. "Seriously, who brings bed sheets when they're going on the run?"

Ananda grunted and shook his head.

"Will you two stop it," said Neel. "Look, we're all hot and thirsty. And so is Ananda. Can we stop wasting our energy on fighting and look for some water?"

"Fine," said Chaya, glaring at Nour. She turned to Neel. "You know what. Ananda will know where the water is. I've heard the mahouts say elephants can smell water from miles away."

"Could that be true?"

"No idea, but it's worth a try." She clapped Ananda on the back. "*Water*, go on. *Water*, Ananda."

Ananda tossed his head, then sped up a little.

"Hang on, Ananda!" said Chaya. "Hey, he's in a hurry. Let's get on."

She hoisted herself up behind Nour, quickly followed by Neel, and Ananda sped them on their way, the sequins on Nour's now dirty clothes blinking in the sunlight.

Soon the trees opened up in front of them and they saw an expanse of water, shimmering a silvery, mirrored green. Ananda bounded towards it.

"Stop him!" Nour shrieked. "He's going straight for the water."

"What did you expect?" shouted Chaya. "I would too."

"But – but, he might drown."

"Elephants can swim, silly."

"No they can't. Stop him!"

"It's true, Nour," said Neel. "Don't worry."

All the same, Nour screamed when Ananda splashed into the river. He glided his way straight into the middle and inhaled a load of water.

Nour screamed again as his humungous head tipped back on to her to drink it.

"Come on," said Neel. "Let's get off."

Ananda inhaled another trunkful of water and his trunk curled up over his head.

The three of them screamed as a heavy shower of water drenched them. They were in hysterics as Ananda showered them again and again as he cooled himself off.

Neel jumped into the river from Ananda's back and Chaya followed. She felt the heat and anger melt away as she splashed Neel with water and he splashed her back.

"Come on in, Nour," said Chaya, throwing water on her. Nour remained on Ananda, but laughed and splashed Chaya back, joining in the water fight while

Ananda lowered himself into the river. She made a huge racket as she splashed and kicked water their way, turning her face to avoid the spray.

"Look, Nour, look at this," said Chaya. She climbed on Ananda, and Nour moved back to make space for her. "*Dip*, Ananda."

Ananda stood up slowly and knelt down on his front legs, dipping his head down in front as Chaya and Nour tilted forwards towards the river. Nour yelped in shock while Chaya slid down Ananda's head and splashed into the river.

"*How* did you do that?" shouted Neel, swimming up to them.

In answer Chaya reached over Ananda's head and vaulted up on to him, and he stood up with her facing his back. "I told you I know all the commands," she shouted, laughing at Neel's astonished face.

"I'm going to have a go," said Neel, getting on Ananda. He tumbled down with a great crash into the river, not at all graceful like Chaya. "Come on, Nour. You too."

"There is *no way* I am doing that," said Nour.

The clearing echoed with their shouts and laughs as they splashed and played around Ananda. Chaya felt worry bubble up inside her as she thought about the King's men coming after them. But she pushed it down for the moment. They had been in fear long enough.

Afterwards they went ashore for food. Chaya went and found two papaya fruits and Neel cut them up with his knife. Ananda sprayed himself with sand, making Nour cry out in dismay.

"*Why* would he do that? He just got clean."

Chaya handed her a chunk of papaya. "It's to keep himself from getting sunburnt."

"No it isn't. Neelan, she's messing with me isn't she?"

Neel laughed. "It's true. The sand also forms a layer of mud that pulls out any bugs on his skin when it falls off."

"I can never tell with you, Chaya." Nour frowned and settled herself against a stone. Chaya laughed.

They sat eating the sweet orange pulp and sunning themselves on the rocks, their clothes drying to a crisp in no time. The sun slipped behind the trees and a warm breeze blew across the water.

"Guess we'll have to get going," said Chaya. "But that was just *great*."

Suddenly Neel frowned. "Did you hear that?"

Nour looked up sleepily. "What? I didn't hear anything."

Neel held up a finger for them to be quiet.

He turned to Chaya and Nour. "Someone's coming."

Chapter Twenty

The jungle felt eerily quiet.

"We can't see anything from here," said Chaya. "Let me climb a tree."

She climbed up a branching *ariddha* tree. A green vine snake slithered down a branch but she ignored it and moved across to a taller tree, hopping from branch to branch until she reached the highest point.

She perched at the top and surveyed her surroundings. From this angle the jungle was a sea of different greens as far as the eye could see, occasionally broken up by a rocky hill.

Nothing looked out of the ordinary. The jungle was full of creatures – she supposed that Neel must have heard one of them. Chaya looked down to the ground and could just about make him out, staring upwards into the tree, with Nour mounted and waiting on Ananda.

It was so calm and still up there. Underneath, the jungle pulsed, but up here it was as if she were the only person in the world.

Then something flashed on a hill to the left. Chaya squinted. There was movement.

Horsemen. Two of them, wiry and fast.

Chaya slid down the branches, tearing her sleeve.

"What took you so long?" said Neel.

"They're coming," said Chaya. "We need to go."

"Come on, quick." Nour moved up Ananda's back to make room for them.

"No, Nour." Chaya's voice broke. "We'll have to leave him."

Nour's mouth fell open.

"They're that close?" said Neel. He rubbed Ananda's side. "Come on, Nour. Down."

Chaya pulled the bags off the elephant and threw them under some bushes. She put her cheek on

Ananda's side and stroked him. "Thank you," she whispered. "For everything. You're going home now."

The first sound of hoof beats echoed through the trees. Chaya followed Neel and Nour as they sprinted off past a startled sambar doe. "Keep together," said Neel. "Whatever you do, don't get separated."

Branches whizzed past them as they pounded through the trees. The hoof beats got closer and Chaya's ankle was starting to throb with a dull pain.

"Come on," Neel called, turning back and grabbing her by the wrist. They plunged down a tiny track, scattering a small troop of purple-faced monkeys.

The hoof beats were deafening now. Chaya stumbled and fell, scratching her legs painfully as Neel dragged her along.

"Nour, wait," said Neel. "We need to stay together."

Trees started rustling behind them. Any minute now the horsemen would be right on their backs. Chaya ignored the pain and sprinted. Neel bolted from behind, and Nour picked up her speed too. They crashed through the wilderness and into a clearing.

They were out in the open for maybe two seconds, but in that time Chaya heard the shout.

The horsemen had seen them.

With a great neighing of horses they galloped closer.

Neel yanked Chaya's hand as they ran off the path into the dense undergrowth. There was no way a horse could follow them here. They heard the clatter and pull-up of hoof beats, and the thud as the two riders dismounted. It gave them the few minutes they needed. Chaya ignored her throbbing ankle and sprinted after Neel. They were single file here, and she saw Nour's red dress flash up ahead, leading them.

In a while, Neel slowed down. Chaya couldn't hear the riders any more. The three of them stopped and Neel held a finger to his lips.

Around them birds sang, a cacophony of raucous sounds. The wind whistled through giant trees and a flying squirrel soared through the air and scuttled up a branch.

"I think we've lost them," whispered Chaya, looking around the deep jungle. "Trouble is, we're completely and utterly lost too."

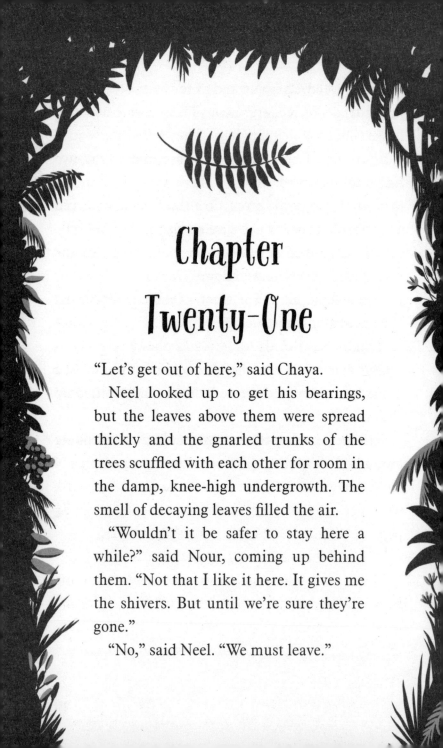

Chapter Twenty-One

"Let's get out of here," said Chaya.

Neel looked up to get his bearings, but the leaves above them were spread thickly and the gnarled trunks of the trees scuffled with each other for room in the damp, knee-high undergrowth. The smell of decaying leaves filled the air.

"Wouldn't it be safer to stay here a while?" said Nour, coming up behind them. "Not that I like it here. It gives me the shivers. But until we're sure they're gone."

"No," said Neel. "We must leave."

Chaya followed Nour and Neel as they squished past a trunk furred with caterpillars towards sparser forest.

Nour yelped and jerked to a stop, making Chaya bump into her.

From the edge of a brook up ahead a leopard stared at them, disturbed while lapping water.

Chaya clamped her hand over Nour's mouth. She held on tightly as Nour struggled to run.

Neel held up his hand. "Keep still. Don't startle it."

The leopard stared keenly at them, its rusty-yellow spotted body reflected in the water.

Chaya took a deep breath to calm herself. She needn't be afraid – man-eaters were rare, despite what she'd told Nour.

Neel took gentle steps forward. He waved a finger over his shoulder for them to follow. Chaya let go of Nour and gave her a light prod. Nour moved forward, whimpering under her breath. Neel took a curving path, staying well out of the way of the leopard.

It turned its head, watching their progress.

Chaya took the shallowest of breaths, making herself as quiet as possible. As long as they didn't make any sudden movements they'd be fine. *Make yourself big, never cower down*, Father had said.

Nour stepped on the hem of her skirt and stumbled to the ground.

The leopard growled and stiffened.

Nour scrabbled about and sprang up with a yowl.

The leopard made a sudden leap.

Nour screamed.

But it had leapt away from them, springing up the bank in one smooth bound and sprinting away into the trees.

Nour burst into tears. "I'm so—"

"Quiet, Nour," said Chaya. "Let's get out of here first."

They walked briskly on, and in ten minutes they were out of the undergrowth and into a drier, less dense part of the forest.

Chaya exhaled. "You nearly got us killed there! Did you seriously think you could outrun a leopard?"

"Go easy on her. She's not used to these things," said Neel. "Nour, we're never out of danger here, all right? We have to stay calm."

Nour nodded, shame-faced and subdued.

Chaya felt a telltale itch on her legs and lifted up the edge of her skirt. A few fat leeches were studded on her shins. Ugh.

"What's that?" said Nour.

Chaya dropped her skirt hurriedly. "Nothing," she said.

Neel frowned at Chaya. She could see a few blots of blood around the bottom of his sarong.

"What are you two hiding from me?" said Nour. She lifted her skirt and at that moment a fat leech dropped down on to her foot.

"It's nothing," said Neel. "Just leeches."

Nour gave a blood-curdling scream that disturbed the monkeys and sent a flock of birds flying into the sky. She stamped her feet and scrabbled at her legs, but Neel pulled her hands off.

"Stop it. It'll only get infected if you pull them off."

"Are you *mad*! I need to get them off!" Nour tried to claw at her legs, but Neel held her arms.

"No, Nour, their mouths will stay embedded in your skin if you do that. *No*."

"So what do I *do*?" Nour stamped and wailed like a demented person.

"They'll drop when they're full. Seriously. Just give it a few minutes."

Chaya sighed. She didn't want to tell Neel she told him so. "We're OK here," she said to Nour. "It's only the dampest parts of the jungle that have them."

Nour looked up at the sky and squeezed her eyes

shut, tears seeping out of them as she wept silently. One by one leeches started dropping from their legs.

"Nour?" Chaya kicked away the blood-gorged lumps of leeches that had fallen off the girl. "You're OK. They're all gone now. Look, you're fine."

Neel looked surprised at Chaya's softer tone. It was almost as if she was starting to feel sorry for Nour.

But Nour pushed Chaya away and stalked ahead. She was properly sobbing now, walking blindly with tears streaming down her face. After a few minutes she stopped and sat on a stone, sobbing down into her lap.

"So *that's* what you wanted s-salt for. I th-thought you wanted to c-*cook*! I h-hate this place. I r-really *hate* this place. This jungle. This country. Everything. Why did I come? I want to go h-home."

Neel went and squatted down near her. "You had no choice. It'll be better whe—"

"I *did* have a choice," screamed Nour. "I d-didn't have to come and you certainly didn't want me to. When the explosion came from the palace all the monks rushed to see what was going on, and I went with them. My f-f-father must be sick with worry, and it's all m-my fault."

Neel looked at Chaya with a frown. Chaya shrugged.

She couldn't understand it either.

"But, Nour, why did you *want* to come?"

"Because I was a f-fool. I wanted to have what you two have." Nour was almost hysterical, muddy streaks down her face and on her blouse. "You're always doing th-th-things. Important, i-interesting things. I don't have any f-friends. Only my father and n-nanny and servants. Nobody else. Not a s-soul. So I made you think I had to c-come with you." She rocked back and forth, head in her hands.

No wonder Nour had looked so guilty earlier. How incredibly *stupid* she had been. This was a life or death situation, and Nour had thrown herself into it because she didn't have friends to do things with.

How lonely must you be to do something like that? This was some level of recklessness, even by Chaya's own standards.

"Nour, listen." Chaya bent down and offered her hand. "We've got to go, come on. We have to get moving."

Nour stared at Chaya's hand, then took it and got up unsteadily.

"We'll talk about this as we go along, OK?" said Neel. "We don't have any time to lose."

Nour nodded shakily. She was still teary and

hiccupy but sniffled and walked along with them.

"Yes, Neel's right." Chaya strode next to her. "We'd better keep moving. The King's going to send all his men into the jungle now that he knows exactly where we are."

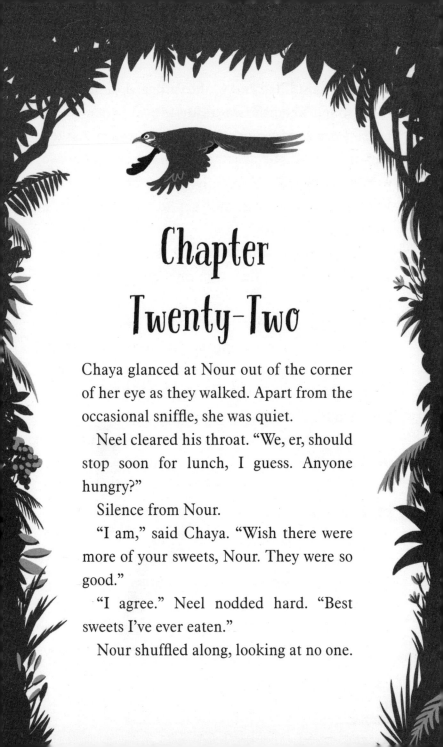

Chapter Twenty-Two

Chaya glanced at Nour out of the corner of her eye as they walked. Apart from the occasional sniffle, she was quiet.

Neel cleared his throat. "We, er, should stop soon for lunch, I guess. Anyone hungry?"

Silence from Nour.

"I am," said Chaya. "Wish there were more of your sweets, Nour. They were so good."

"I agree." Neel nodded hard. "Best sweets I've ever eaten."

Nour shuffled along, looking at no one.

Neel caught Chaya's eye. She shrugged. Nour would come round when she was ready.

"How much off course do you think we are?" asked Chaya.

Neel shrugged. "Hopefully not much. If we keep heading south we can still get to Galle, just by a slightly longer route."

Chaya's heart sank. Now the guards knew they were in the jungle, they wouldn't stop searching till they found them.

They stopped near a river and sat down on some large rocks, Nour staying as far away from them on the bank as possible. Neel got into the river and walked ahead, trying to catch the darting fish with his bare hands.

Chaya wandered over to Nour and tried to get a fire going with two rocks and a few sticks the way Neel had done. But five minutes later she was still bashing them together, and even after smashing a bit of a thumb hadn't got so much as a spark. She turned to Nour and wiped her hair away from her sweaty forehead. "Do you know how to do this, Nour? I wish I'd watched when Neel was doing it."

Nour shook her head without looking at Chaya.

Chaya threw the stones into the river, where they

bounced on a rock and splashed into the water.

"Do you think he's all right?" asked Nour in a small voice.

"Who? Neel?" Chaya turned to see him splashing about in the water.

"Not Neelan. The elephant."

"Oh." Chaya shrugged. "The King's men would have taken him back home. Which is the best thing for him, really. Since, you know, he's been brought up in captivity."

Nour nodded.

Neel came clambering up to them, carrying two glistening silver fish. "Thought you might have a fire going."

"I – we tried, but it didn't work. Come on, Nour. Let's get Neel some more sticks for the fire."

Nour got up slowly and followed her. Chaya collected branches and laid them in a pile, and Nour made trips back and forth, taking them to Neel.

"I think that's enough now." Chaya threw the last of the sticks into the pile.

Nour gently poked some plants with her shoe. "Have you seen this? The leaves fold up when you touch them!"

"And they straighten out soon after." Chaya came

over to Nour. "They're called touch-me-nots. Not a big deal, they're just weeds."

"Strange." Nour touched different parts over and over, watching the leaves curl up, then straighten out again. "The world is full of amazing things. Plants that can feel, elephants that can swim, squirrels that can fly. I wish I knew all this stuff."

"You'll learn."

"I know. I've got to know so much already." Nour looked up at Chaya. "I was wondering, could you teach me to climb trees?"

"Sure."

Nour smiled. "Thanks. I've just thought of what we can do if we see another leopard. We just climb a tree!"

Chaya sighed.

"Hey!" Neel yelled. He had stuck the two fish on a stick and was holding it over a fire. "Do I have to do everything around here?"

Chaya scrambled up and took over from Neel. He went off and sat in the shade, fashioning a sort of pitcher out of wood.

It was scorching near the fire. Smoke curled around the fish and singed at Chaya's fingers. "How long do you think I need to hold it like this?"

Nour shrugged. "Until it looks cooked?"

Chaya held it closer to the flames.

"Wait," said Nour. "I'm sure that should be enough now."

"Yeah, this should be OK. It looks nicely coloured."

"*Coloured?*" Neel came over and slapped his forehead. "Those look burnt."

"They probably *taste* good." Chaya put them on leaves and passed one to Neel. "And that's all that matters.

She broke off a piece and took a bite. "Eurgh."

Neel spat out his mouthful.

Nour put hers down without so much as a nibble.

"Honestly, it was a simple task." Neel rubbed the back of his hand on his tongue. "Do I have to do everything?"

"It's not a big deal." Chaya got up and tossed the charred fish away. "Let me find some fruit or something."

"People make mistakes, Neelan," said Nour, shaking her head at a surprised Neel. She stood up and went with Chaya. "I'll help you look."

"Oh." Chaya was at a loss for words. "Thank you."

They went off to find some food together.

Chapter
Twenty-Three

"How much further is Galle?" Nour's face was red and sweaty as she shuffled along next to Chaya.

"I think we're about halfway there," said Neel.

Nour groaned.

"Once we're out of the jungle we'll be OK," said Chaya. "I mean, we could hitch a ride on a cart or something then?" She looked hopefully at Neel.

"Yes, I'm sure we'll find something. It's important to keep moving now, and put as much distance as possible between us and where we were seen last."

"And we need to make up for that whole detour we took," said Chaya.

"I wish we could have another break," said Nour. "I'm dying."

"Oh come on, don't be such a wimp," said Chaya.

"Five minutes. Please." Nour sagged down on a tree stump.

Neel glanced at Chaya. "Let's give her five minutes."

"Fine. Just five. And counting."

Chaya picked at some wild mint leaves while they waited, crushing them in her fingers and inhaling their aroma. A squashed-looking owl the colour of dried leaves roosted in a branch overhead.

Neel handed Nour the pitcher of water he was carrying and she drank greedily.

"Thank you," she whispered.

"Wait a minute." Neel held up a hand and listened intently. "Oh no. Not again."

Chaya pricked up her ears. All she heard was the twitch of the owl and rustling of leaves.

"They're here," said Neel. "Come on. Nour, get up."

Chaya looked back. They could see only about thirty feet behind them. "I don't hear anything," she said.

"Trust me, they're here. They've got to be close."

With a great sound of hooves, horsemen erupted into view in the distance. Neel was off like a hare, pulling Nour by her wrist. Chaya sprinted after them. The jungle was sparse here, the horses easily catching up with them.

Chaya vaulted over a fallen tree. She saw Nour's dress flash ahead and kept up with her. The thuds of horse hooves were getting closer. She knew Nour was already tired. It was only minutes before they'd be captured, surely.

The horsemen were practically at her back. The hoof beats vibrated through Chaya, pounding into her head. She burst ahead, almost passing Nour but slowed down for her.

She couldn't see Neel anywhere.

"Where's Neel?" Chaya screamed. Nour looked around in terror, but kept on ahead. The horsemen seemed to have divided, some of them going off in another direction.

Chaya looked around wildly. A group of horsemen were chasing something on the far left. They disappeared from sight as she pounded after Nour, a small army of guards at their back.

Chaya and Nour were alone in the jungle, being

chased by the King's guards.

And Neel was gone.

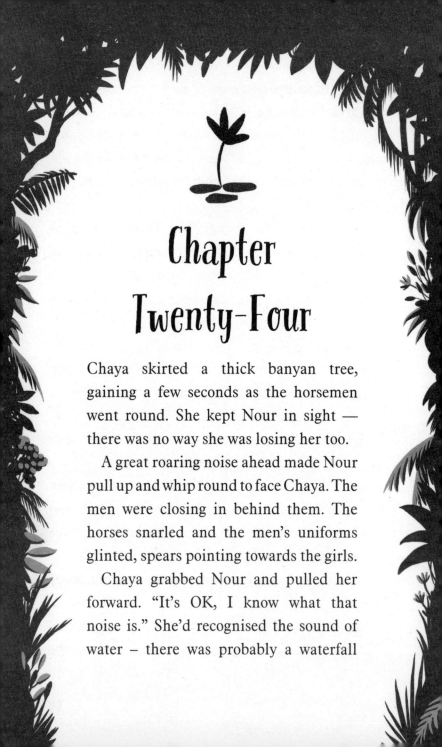

Chapter Twenty-Four

Chaya skirted a thick banyan tree, gaining a few seconds as the horsemen went round. She kept Nour in sight — there was no way she was losing her too.

A great roaring noise ahead made Nour pull up and whip round to face Chaya. The men were closing in behind them. The horses snarled and the men's uniforms glinted, spears pointing towards the girls.

Chaya grabbed Nour and pulled her forward. "It's OK, I know what that noise is." She'd recognised the sound of water – there was probably a waterfall up ahead. "Come on."

A warm spray hit Chaya as she ran on with Nour. Behind them the men got closer. There was a rank, leathery smell from the horses, puffs of dust in the air, and ahead of them, from somewhere they couldn't yet see, mists of water.

They rounded the corner and there it was. A gigantic waterfall, crashing and roaring. Curtains of pure-white water gushed down, falling far below into an aquamarine pool. The girls were drenched as soon as they stepped on to the ledge.

They were cornered. From behind them came the gallop of horses as the men rounded the bend. Chaya looked down into the pool. It was almost circular at the bottom, broad and clear, before thinning into a long strip of churning river. There was only one option. The pool looked deep enough.

"Jump, Nour!" she screamed over the roaring water.

Nour stared at her in fright, her hair hanging in wet strings round her face. "No," she shrieked, her voice swallowed by the crashing of the water.

The horsemen approached slowly, wearing smug expressions.

"Nour, it's safe," yelled Chaya. "Nour, listen to me."

But Nour didn't react. She stared wildly from the

men and back to the waterfall.

They couldn't get caught now. The King would have them put to death at once.

Chaya reached out and pushed Nour into the waterfall.

Nour's scream died on her lips as she tipped down into the abyss of crashing water.

Chaya jumped in after her.

She felt herself whistle through the air before plunging into the water below and slicing down into its cool, swirling depths. The deafening roar muted as she plummeted to the sandy bottom. She kicked hard and surfaced quickly into the rumble and spray, looking around for Nour through hair plastered across her eyes. The current pulled her down the river with the gushing water.

Eventually she was spat into a narrow stream of water. Where was Nour? The water was fast-flowing, but the river was narrow here and the banks were fairly close. Chaya looked up and saw the ledge they'd jumped from high above her. It would take at least half an hour for the men and their horses to find their way down by land.

Something brownish pushed past her downriver, and a cold fear seized Chaya. A crocodile, here? She struck out towards the shore, hitting her palms on rocks as she struggled against the flow. The brown thing rushed ahead, and Chaya saw a white hand loll out on the side. She squinted at it through the mist. It wasn't a crocodile.

It was Nour.

Chaya struck out towards her. Why wasn't Nour making for the shore?

"Nour!" she screamed. "Nour!"

A memory came back to her. "*Is it deep?*" Nour had asked about the river. Her screaming on top of Ananda, "*He's going straight for the water.*" And she'd stayed on his back the whole time they'd swum in the river.

Nour was scared of water and probably couldn't swim. And Chaya had just pushed her down an eighty-foot waterfall.

Chapter
Twenty-Five

Chaya thrashed towards Nour. She would save her if it was the last thing she did. The water surged and crashed around her. She fought to close the distance between them. She had always been a strong swimmer but the river was rough and wild.

"Nour!" she yelled again. "Nour!"

But Nour didn't respond. Her body flopped ahead in the waves. Was she even conscious?

Chaya felt a stab of fear. She kicked out furiously. "Nour. I'm coming."

The gap between them was wider than ever. It was useless. Neel was missing, probably still in the jungle area where they'd jumped. Maybe captured by the King's men. And Nour was dying in the water. It was all her fault. Again and again and again, it was all because of her.

She kicked and thrashed and swam towards Nour. She was getting closer, so close now Chaya could almost reach out and touch her. Chaya launched herself at Nour, grabbing at her clothes as they hurtled along.

Nour was conscious, but barely. Her eyes showed a flicker of recognition but she was too exhausted to move. Chaya struggled to tug Nour ashore, but she wasn't helping. She slumped like a dead weight in Chaya's arms.

"Nour, we need to get to the shore. Please. Work with me."

She grunted as she fought against the current to drag Nour to the bank.

Rocky ledges speckled the sandy banks of the river. Chaya tried to lift Nour on to one of them.

She shoved Nour upwards towards a flattish rock. She had to get Nour out of the water and on land. Chaya felt her strength fading away. The sun burned at her head and spots swam in front of her eyes. She had to save Nour. If Nour fell back into the water Chaya wouldn't have the strength to help her again.

She gave one last heave and rolled Nour on to the ledge, where she moaned and lay still. Chaya tried to hoist herself after Nour, but her arms had seized up. The brightness of the day dimmed into black shadows, and the last thing she saw was the water closing over her face as she fainted backwards into the water.

Chapter Twenty-Six

Chaya was in a deep sleep. Everything was peaceful here. The sound of birdsong mingled with the swishing of leaves and gush of water. Then something thick and warm wrapped itself around Chaya's waist as she was lifted high into the air.

Her body made contact with something hard and she was shaken awake.

Chaya's clothes and hair were soaked and clinging to her. Her cheek was pressed against a flat rock. She opened her mouth and vomited out water. Over and over again, until she felt light and worn out.

She opened her eyes.

The river lay in front of her, swirling and white. Above her the blue sky arced over the horizon. A large butterfly with black and white markings on translucent wings fluttered past, its shadow crossing her face as it went.

Was this real? Or had she drowned?

If she had, she deserved it.

Neel was gone.

And thanks to her, Nour was alone too.

All of them lost in Serendib's jungle.

A chilly wind swept her wet body and she shivered. Her arms stung from the cuts all over them. Chaya lifted her head and looked down at herself. Her tattered clothes clung to her and an enormous shadow fell across her legs.

That shadow. There was something familiar about it.

Chaya lifted herself up on her elbows, wincing as she did so. She turned to look behind her.

There, his huge tusks looming over her, stood Ananda.

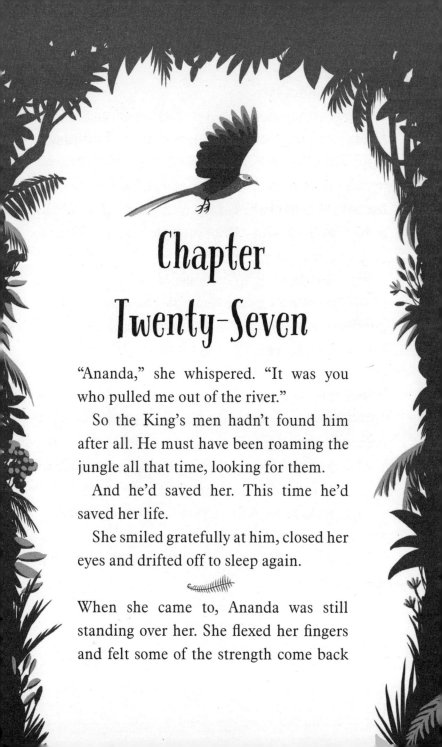

Chapter Twenty-Seven

"Ananda," she whispered. "It was you who pulled me out of the river."

So the King's men hadn't found him after all. He must have been roaming the jungle all that time, looking for them.

And he'd saved her. This time he'd saved her life.

She smiled gratefully at him, closed her eyes and drifted off to sleep again.

When she came to, Ananda was still standing over her. She flexed her fingers and felt some of the strength come back to her limbs.

Chaya sat up shakily and pulled herself to her feet. It was evening. The sky was darkening and the jungle was full of the shrieks of crickets.

"We need to find them, Ananda," she said. She looked along the banks of the river but no flash of red dress caught her eye. "Nour must be here somewhere. And we need to find Neel."

She sank down on to her knees and buried her face in her lap. Who was she fooling? The jungle rose up around her, a vast swathe of darkness and light, and Neel and Nour were two pinpricks lost somewhere in it.

Something wrapped itself like a blanket around her middle, and once again she found herself lifted up in Ananda's trunk and on to his broad back. She felt the warmth of him like an embrace and the lull of his gait as he thumped his way along the riverbank.

She rubbed the back of her hand over her eyes. "Nour?" she called out.

Ananda padded on, stepping over weeds and through flat ground.

"*Nour*. Can you hear me?"

She urged Ananda on. "She can't be too far off. Nour! Neel? Do you hear me?"

Her shouts echoed through the jungle. A civet stopped in its tracks and then scuttled away, its golden body quivering in the waning light.

Where were they? And where were the King's men? Would *they* hear her?

"Nour!"

Ananda lifted up his head and trumpeted. The sound boomed through the forest and was met by a whispering of trees as owls woke up and hooted. Followed by another cry. Softer.

Human.

There was a movement ahead. Chaya squinted into the gloom. Something was coming towards them.

And there in the distance, framed by a giant split ironwood tree, was Nour.

"I thought I'd never find you," said Nour, hobbling towards Chaya. Her eyes were swollen and her face streaked with dirt. "First, Neelan. Then you." A fresh outpouring of tears coursed down her face.

Chaya jumped off Ananda and hugged Nour. "I'm so sorry. I didn't know."

"Know what?" Nour sniffed and rubbed her eyes. She looked worn through.

"About the water. That, you know…"

"That I'm a coward who's afraid of everything?"

Nour laughed, before her body was racked by a sob.

"I shouldn't have pushed you."

"Never mind. It saved us, didn't it? Otherwise we'd be with the King by now. Being put to the sword for helping a criminal escape."

"Still. I'm sorry. I know it's not enough."

Nour shook her head. "Do you think they got Neelan?"

"I hope not. He might have escaped. He was ahead of us. Neel can be quick when he has to be."

"What do we do now?"

"We look for Neel."

"But if we stay here the King's men will find us. And if we go too far we won't find Neel." Nour started to sob again. "Oh, Chaya, it's hopeless, isn't it?"

"No it isn't." There was no need to make things worse than it was. "We need to stay strong, Nour."

Chaya couldn't navigate the jungle like Neel did. She had no idea where they were.

"How big is this jungle?" asked Nour.

"Er, not very." She felt terrible for lying, but now wasn't the time to reveal that the jungle covered nearly half of Serendib. "We can do this. Come on, you ride Ananda. We'll find somewhere to settle for the night, and then look for Neel in the morning, OK?"

Nour nodded. "It's a good thing we found Ananda," she said. She smiled up at him but didn't touch him. At least she was using his name now.

Ananda kneeled and Nour clambered on to him. Chaya led them away from the river and into the trees.

The jungle was much cooler now. The sun was setting and the gaps between trees darkened into hollows. Chaya and Nour swapped places as they went on.

"Do you wish," said Nour from where she was walking along, munching on a piece of grass, "that you could go back and undo everything?"

"What kind of silly question is that?"

"Well, think about it. You would be safe. Neel would be safe. Your father would continue on as before. Everything would be the same. But Vijay would lose his leg and never walk again."

"I'm tired. Do I have to answer these questions?"

"I'm tired too. But it passes the time. I just wondered, that's all. You don't have to answer." Then Nour added under her breath, "Especially since you never admit you're wrong."

Chaya ignored her. The truth was, she wasn't sure any more.

They swapped again as they looked for a place to

settle for the night. After a while, Chaya led Ananda to a halt under a canopy of trees, with a springy bed of ferns underneath. "This looks comfortable enough."

Nour looked around sadly as she got off Ananda. "We can't even have a fire without Neelan."

"We've got Ananda," said Chaya. "No animal would come close with him protecting us." She hoped that was true.

"I have something to tell you," said Nour. "I think I'm dying."

Chaya raised an eyebrow.

"You could be a bit more sympathetic." Nour pulled back her sleeve and showed her arm. "Look at all these pink spots. I have them all over me."

"Nour, I hate to tell you the obvious, but we're in a jungle. Those are insect bites."

Nour pulled a face. "That's horrible. How come you don't have them? Or Neel."

"Of course I have them, but why would it bother me? That's the least of our worries right now." She looked round at the trees. "Let's find something to eat."

"I wish I could climb trees like you," said Nour, looking up into the branches of a thick tree.

"I'll show you soon, I promise. Just need to get

something to eat now."

"I mean, there's that prickly fruit up there in the tree." She pointed up into the branches. "There, look."

Chaya looked up, following Nour's finger. "It's a jackfruit! That's the best fruit ever!"

Nour smiled and sat cross-legged on the ferns as Chaya shimmied up the tree to pick the juiciest jackfruit she could find.

They might as well enjoy the moment. Because tomorrow they had the impossible task of finding Neel in this gigantic jungle.

Chapter Twenty-Eight

"Nour," Chaya whispered, and shook her. Dawn had broken, and shafts of light thrummed from between the trees.

Nour moaned and stretched. "It's morning already?"

"Shh." Chaya looked around. "I think they're coming. We need to get going."

Nour grimaced and staggered to her feet.

"We'll both ride Ananda. Come on."

Chaya dragged her stiff body up behind Nour and they swayed softly as Ananda moved off. From behind them came a faint hum, like a swarm of moths. Something about the sound, the puffs of dust drifting through, the tension in the air, told Chaya something big was coming towards them.

But Ananda was doing a good job of running away from it all, as he hurtled through the trees at top speed.

"I think we've lost them," shouted Chaya, slowing Ananda down. "I don't hear anything now."

"You know, once this is all over, we should give Ananda a huge treat. What's an elephant treat?"

"I don't know." Chaya glanced behind them. "Sugar cane maybe."

"You know so much stuff," said Nour as they rode under a banyan tree, its trailing leaves brushing against their legs. "How did you learn these things?"

Chaya shrugged. "It's just *stuff*. Everyone knows them." She noticed Nour's frown. "You're different. You're new here. You'll get to know things soon enough."

Nour was silent for a bit. "I thought you were going to laugh at me," she said. "That's what the old you would have done."

Something whizzed past Chaya's ear and an arrow stabbed into a tree. Nour screamed.

Chaya tapped Ananda on his side and he sped up, thundering through the trees. Another arrow came whistling past, this time ripping through one of Nour's sleeves.

"Oh no, they're here, they're here!" Nour screamed.

"Calm down, Nour," said Chaya. She needed to think. Something wasn't as it should be.

There was no sound of galloping. Were the King's men now on foot?

Nour screamed and pointed behind them. "Look at that! *What* are those?"

They were squelching through a muddy patch where several man-sized water lizards were glistening blackly. Ananda just stepped over the scaly creatures and their whiplash tails.

"They're called water monitors. And they're horrible," said Chaya as they zipped away from the creatures. She turned back to look in front of her and screamed. "*Duck*, Nour!"

They both bobbed down just in time to avoid the thick horizontal branch whistling towards them.

"Better keep our eyes in front!" called Chaya.

Nour nodded, her eyes fixed ahead.

Ananda suddenly slowed down, even though Chaya tapped him and urged him on. But he eased right down to a plod.

"What's the matter with Ananda?" she said to Nour. But then she looked to where Nour was silently pointing.

Standing on the forest floor ahead of them was a man with a bow, his arrow trained straight at them.

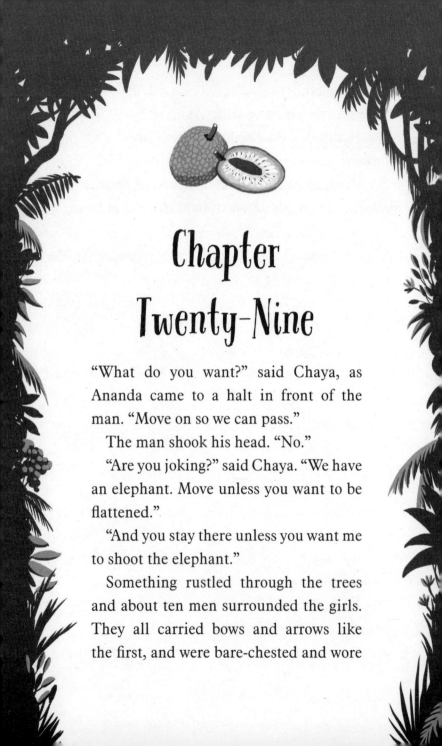

Chapter Twenty-Nine

"What do you want?" said Chaya, as Ananda came to a halt in front of the man. "Move on so we can pass."

The man shook his head. "No."

"Are you joking?" said Chaya. "We have an elephant. Move unless you want to be flattened."

"And you stay there unless you want me to shoot the elephant."

Something rustled through the trees and about ten men surrounded the girls. They all carried bows and arrows like the first, and were bare-chested and wore dirty sarongs tied up to their knees. Chaya stared at them.

Bandits!

"We've been waiting for you," said the first man. He seemed like the leader, and looked slightly less scruffy than the rest. "We have something of yours."

Something of *theirs*? Whatever did he mean?

There was more rustling through the bushes, and someone else emerged.

"Neel!" Chaya slid off Ananda and threw her arms around the bedraggled Neel, followed by Nour, who did the same. "*Neel*. Are you OK?"

The bandit holding Neel rolled his eyes and Neel blushed furiously. He gave the girls an awkward pat and untangled himself hastily. "Yes, I'm fine. I'm so glad to see you."

The men gathered round Ananda, and one tried to rub his hide. Ananda swayed and shook his head.

"Hey, what are you doing?" yelled Chaya. "He doesn't like that."

"We're taking him," said the bandit leader. "Why do you think we were waiting for you?"

"Gamage," said Neel to the leader. "The elephant's getting agitated. Someone could get hurt."

"Lead him to our place then, boy," said Gamage,

backing away from a sidestepping Ananda. "We can chain him up until he's used to us."

"Why would we do that!" said Chaya. "Get away now, before he mows you down."

Gamage turned to them. "Listen, children. We'd rather kill this beast right now and take his tusks if we had our way. But we have orders to take him unhurt. So help us and nothing need happen to him."

"Orders?" said Chaya. "From whom?"

"Stop asking questions!" Gamage looked irritated as the other men stepped back from Ananda, whose massive body kept moving from side to side. Something crunched under the elephant's foot, sending the men retreating even further. "If the animal keeps doing this we'll have no choice but to shoot."

Chaya darted up to Ananda and shooed the men away. Slowly he calmed down as he saw the three of them, even rubbing his trunk on Neel's head.

Neel rubbed him on the back. "I missed you too, Ananda."

"Heart-warming as this reunion is," said Gamage, "we need to be taking the elephant now. So if you'll lead him our way, it's in your – and the animal's – best interest. Try anything and we'll shoot."

Chaya glanced at Neel and he nodded slightly. They

didn't want Ananda to be hurt.

"We'll bring him," said Neel.

The men led the way, all the while looking suspiciously at the children.

They followed Gamage and his men to a kind of jungle hideout. Little wooden huts squatted low among smaller trees in a clearing, and on a central platform a few other men sat smoking and chatting.

Neel dropped his voice to a whisper. "The news from Nirissa isn't good. I've been hearing a few things while I've been here. Apparently the King is terrorising the villagers, asking them to give us up. They haven't stopped since we left. The people are frightened and angry. They hate us too because of what we've brought on them. They don't ever want us to return."

Chaya staggered backwards and leaned against Ananda.

"Do you know if our families are safe?" said Nour. She'd stuffed the back of her fingers in her mouth.

"I'm not sure, but nobody in the village…" Neel looked away and swallowed. "Nobody is dead."

A *yet* hovered unsaid in the air.

"Father would try to reason with the King," said Chaya. "He'd do his best for the village."

"I – I don't think he can do much at the moment," said Neel.

"Why not? He'd do anything for the villagers."

Neel looked absolutely miserable. "He's been arrested, Chaya."

Chapter Thirty

Chaya was speechless. The village was in turmoil and Father in jail. Things couldn't get any worse than this.

Nour hurriedly changed the topic, as if that would make Chaya forget. "Why did the bandits take you, Neelan?"

"They wanted me to lead them to you and Ananda."

"They must want him for his tusks," said Nour.

"No, they were telling the truth. They do want him alive and unhurt."

"It's probably to sell him on." She

exchanged worried glances with Neel.

Chaya stared ahead towards the platform. Her village was in danger and she needed some time to think. Gamage and the men were sitting on their haunches, talking to the others.

"They want him for Sena, the King's half-brother," said Neel.

"*What?*" Chaya was stunned. She turned her full attention to Neel. "So it's true? The banished prince really is back for the throne?"

"Yes, and these men are on his side. Ananda is the King's elephant, the state elephant. They want him alive for Sena."

"So that some day Sena can ride in to victory on the King's elephant?"

Neel nodded.

"I can't believe it," said Nour. "He's actually back. This must be the King's worst nightmare come true."

"It wouldn't be for months yet that they try to do anything," said Neel. "Sena's people are collecting supporters bit by bit in different parts of the island."

"What about round your village?" said Nour.

"Not yet. They are slowly working their way inwards towards the King's City."

"Wait a minute." A plan was beginning to take

shape in Chaya's head. "Does this mean these men are enemies of the King?"

"Yes," said Neel. "He must hate them more than he hates us."

"And that's saying something," said Nour.

The plan was growing and strengthening, and seeming more and more plausible all the time. "Am I the only one seeing a way out of all this and saving our people at the same time?"

Nour looked puzzled.

"What do you mean?" said Neel.

"Oh, Neel, don't you see? Any enemy of the King is a best friend to us."

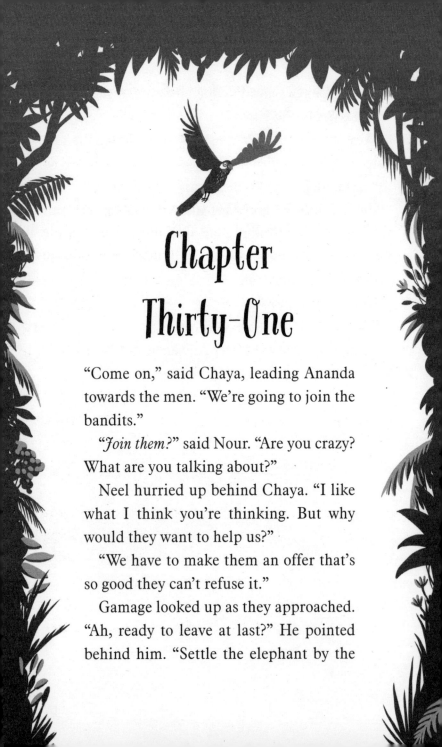

Chapter Thirty-One

"Come on," said Chaya, leading Ananda towards the men. "We're going to join the bandits."

"*Join them?*" said Nour. "Are you crazy? What are you talking about?"

Neel hurried up behind Chaya. "I like what I think you're thinking. But why would they want to help us?"

"We have to make them an offer that's so good they can't refuse it."

Gamage looked up as they approached. "Ah, ready to leave at last?" He pointed behind him. "Settle the elephant by the tree. Would you like some food before you go?"

"Thank you, that'd be good," said Chaya. She came up and sat down on the platform with Nour.

Gamage shouted something at a man inside one of the huts, and he came out bringing bowls of manioc and wood apples that he set down in front of them.

Chaya broke the shell and dug into a wood apple hungrily. "So you steal for a living?" she said to Gamage.

He looked amused. "You could say that."

"And you're loyal to Sena?"

"I see the boy has updated you very quickly. Yes."

"How do you win supporters for him?"

"Most people hate the King, so it's not that difficult," said Gamage. "But even so, it's harder than you'd think. We employ some ... less than noble tactics sometimes."

"Like what?" said Nour.

Gamage shrugged. "We loot villages to make the people feel unsafe. It turns them against the King because he's supposed to look after them. That way, they're more open to someone new stepping in."

"Sena pays you to do these things?" Chaya took a swig of water from a clay pitcher. "I thought he was a good person."

"I don't think he knows everything we do. What matters is winning supporters, and getting rid of the King. Very few people have even seen Sena. He has trusted advisers who handle everything."

"Well, that's all very interesting," said Chaya. She cleared her throat. "We have an offer for you."

Gamage snorted. "An offer of what? We weren't asking nicely for the elephant. We would have taken it anyway."

"We want to join you."

Gamage laughed outright at that. "Why would we *want* you?"

"I think we'd be a big asset to you. We can directly help Sena in his victory."

Gamage stared at Chaya. "Confident child, aren't you? I don't like this kind of grand talk. I think you should clear out now."

"We can help," insisted Chaya. "You do know what we did, right? We may be children, but do you know anyone else who could steal the Queen's jewels from a place as heavily guarded as the royal palace? Someone who walked right into the Queen's quarters?"

Gamage grinned and shook his head, but she could tell he was impressed.

"*And* got one of the King's prisoners out of jail,"

said Neel.

"Actually all of them, if we're counting," said Chaya.

Gamage inclined his head, amused, as if conceding a point.

"And stole the King's elephant," said Nour, catching on.

"All right, all right! But why would you want to help us?"

"We want to save our people in Nirissa."

Gamage snorted. "Your people hate you. You're not going to get any hero's welcome there."

"We don't care about that," said Chaya. "Our people have suffered too long at the King's hands. Think about it. Nirissa is right on the doorstep of the King's City. And this is the *perfect* time to strike."

"I don't make those decisions, girl," said Gamage. "We take our orders from Prince Sena."

"Then take us to meet Sena and we can discuss this with him ourselves."

Gamage threw back his head and laughed. He was still shaking with mirth when he spoke. "Like I said, confident child, aren't you? You can join us if you like; your skills might be useful to us. But if you think that Prince Sena will be interested in any of you or your grand ideas you can forget it right now."

Nour put down her plate and leaned in towards Gamage. "Without the support of the surrounding villages like Nirissa, Sena can never succeed. Imagine what he could do if all the men and women joined him as he marched in? And support for the King right now is the *lowest* it has ever been. If Sena misses this opportunity, another one might not come for a very long time."

Chaya sat back casually. "And *you* could be the one who spotted this chance. I'm sure Sena would be very grateful."

Gamage stared at the three of them as if trying to figure out what to make of them. Finally he relented. "I'll pass on the message to those who give me orders."

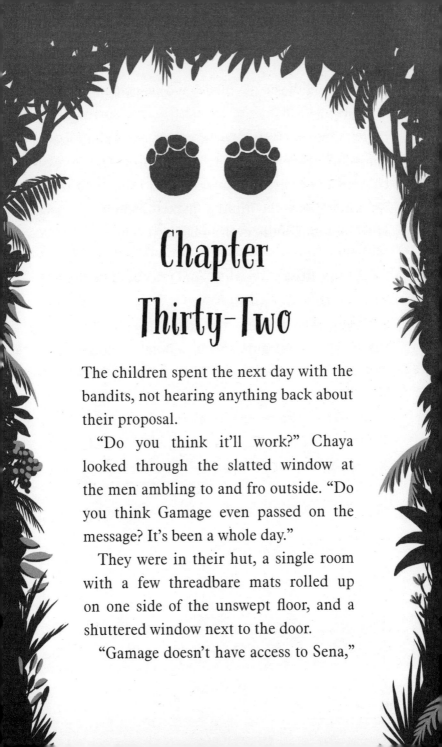

Chapter Thirty-Two

The children spent the next day with the bandits, not hearing anything back about their proposal.

"Do you think it'll work?" Chaya looked through the slatted window at the men ambling to and fro outside. "Do you think Gamage even passed on the message? It's been a whole day."

They were in their hut, a single room with a few threadbare mats rolled up on one side of the unswept floor, and a shuttered window next to the door.

"Gamage doesn't have access to Sena,"

said Neel. "It has to go through others and reach him wherever he is."

"Sena must know about us if he knew about Ananda." Nour was sitting on the pile of mats, her chin on her knees and hugging her legs. "And what we said about the timing makes complete sense. He'd be a fool not to even consider it."

"We're running out of time," said Chaya. What would the King do with Father? "How long can we wait for Sena to respond?"

Nour picked at a stray thread on the mat beside her. "Aren't you two afraid? This is so much … bigger than I thought it would be. This is an actual *war* with the King."

"It was going to happen anyway," said Chaya. "With a king like ours, and with Sena back to stake his claim. But our people need it *right now*."

"But what if the villagers are hostile?" said Nour. "They've suffered so much because of us. Why would they be jumping at a war with the King?"

"We'll just have to convince them," said Neel. "There's no turning back now."

Gamage summoned them later that evening. The men were gathered on the platform around a blazing fire over which fish hung to roast.

"Come, come. Have a bit of dinner with us," said Gamage when he saw them. "Sit down." He gestured at some men sitting nearby as if he were sweeping rubbish away with a broom, and they moved off to the side. "Had a good rest?"

"Yes, thank you," said Neel, sitting down.

The air was warm and smoky. Pots of toddy were being carried in, and the men were getting slightly raucous. In the background Ananda's shape loomed through the darkness and smoke, still tethered under the tree.

"So tell me about home," said Gamage, as a man came up with a wooden tray of whole roasted fish. "You all live in Nirissa?"

"Neel and I do." Chaya took one from the proffered tray. "Nour lives in the King's City itself."

"And you have knowledge of the palace?"

"Of course." Chaya bit into the fish. These were soft and spicy, unlike the ones they'd burnt at the river. "Not to blow our own conch shell, but we did get in there twice. Once to the Queen's quarters, and once to the underground prison complex. We work as a team. We each have our, er, talents."

"I see." Gamage nodded and turned to Neel. "And

you must be the mastermind. Tell me, boy, how did you do it?"

Chaya bristled.

"I... I, er... I didn't... It wasn't... I mean." Neel cleared his throat. "It just ... happened."

Gamage shook his head. "You don't want to part with your secrets, I see. But it's OK, I have some news for you."

Around them the men talked and laughed and munched their food, their faces tinged orange in the firelight. A man came round at the end with a large pot of buffalo curd that everyone dug into with glee.

"What news?" Chaya put down her tin plate, hardly daring to hope.

"You've got your wish. Prince Sena wants to see you."

Chapter
Thirty-Three

The next day they set out early, walking briskly through the jungle with Gamage. He seemed to know his way very well, and by midday they'd come to the edge of the forest, where a cart was waiting.

Chaya hoisted herself up after the others into the cart. "This is nice. I thought we were going to walk all the way."

"Prince Sena is living with a friend of his family," said Gamage, sitting opposite them. "Someone close to his mother's side, who's always been loyal to them."

They didn't talk much after that with

Gamage sitting beside them. It was refreshing being out in open country after being in the jungle so long, the blue sky endless above them. The cart trundled down the coastal road, coconut trees flashing past as they drew on towards Sena.

They drove through a pair of gates down a curving drive, and stopped at a large many-gabled house with a latticed porch and wide verandah.

A man was standing outside, immaculate in starched clothes and slicked hair and moustache. "I'm Mangala," he said to them. "Please go and sit down, I'll be with you in a minute."

Chaya and Nour followed Neel inside, while Mangala stayed back and had a few words with Gamage. All the doors into the house from the verandah were thrown wide open against the walls, and the place was bright and airy, even grander than Nour's, with very high ceilings and plants flowing here and there through railings and winding around posts.

"This is nice," said Chaya, sitting on the polished railing seat of the verandah and leaning out. "Somehow I thought Sena would be locked away somewhere hidden."

They watched the cart roll away down the gravel

drive as Gamage left. Mangala nodded at them as he walked in, and showed them to a carved settee. It felt strange to be sitting on proper seats, and having cups of coriander tea served to them on silver trays.

"I hope you had a comfortable ride," said Mangala. "You can have some rest before lunch."

"Can we have a bath too?" said Nour. "Please."

"Of course."

"When do we meet Sena?" said Chaya. "We'd like to speak to him as soon as possible."

"I understand," said Mangala. "You will meet this evening, after you've washed and eaten. I should let you know … he might not be … what you're expecting."

"What do you mean?" said Neel.

Chaya exchanged a glance with Neel. Gamage hadn't seen Sena either. He'd said very few people had. What was Mangala saying? She didn't care if he had two heads, as long as he wasn't like the King.

But Mangala shook his head mysteriously and even looked amused. "You'll find out."

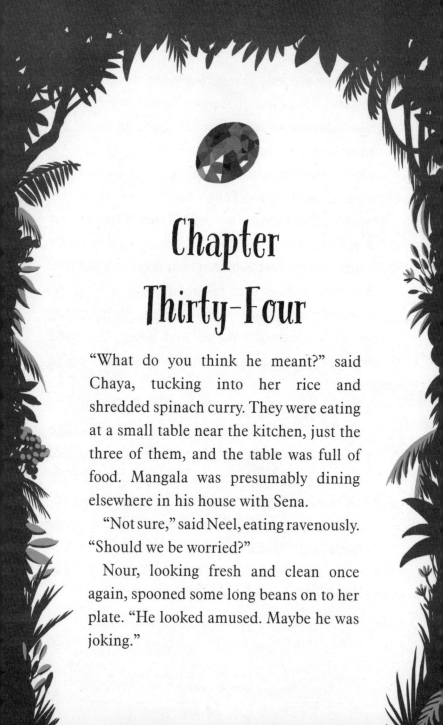

Chapter Thirty-Four

"What do you think he meant?" said Chaya, tucking into her rice and shredded spinach curry. They were eating at a small table near the kitchen, just the three of them, and the table was full of food. Mangala was presumably dining elsewhere in his house with Sena.

"Not sure," said Neel, eating ravenously. "Should we be worried?"

Nour, looking fresh and clean once again, spooned some long beans on to her plate. "He looked amused. Maybe he was joking."

"He doesn't seem like a joking type," said Chaya.

"Let's not set too much store by Sena." Neel pushed the dhal towards Nour, who was reaching for it. "If he doesn't want to do this we'll have to try something else. Go back to Nirissa maybe, and help them somehow."

"It's going to be hard to defend ourselves against the *King*," said Chaya. "It would be so much easier with Sena and his army of supporters on our side."

"The fact that we're here means he's interested," said Nour.

"Let's just see what he says." Chaya poured herself a glass of king-coconut water and took a sip. "Aah, that was delicious."

Mangala peeped into the room and tapped on the side of the door. "All finished here? If you're ready, Sena will see you now."

"Yes, coming," said Chaya. They scrambled up quickly and followed him through the living room to another wing of the house. At last.

"Remember, children, this is the true monarch of Serendib, who will, with the help of the people, take the throne soon. Be respectful all the time. Even if …" Mangala hesitated, "he doesn't demand it."

Mangala stopped at a pair of double doors and

knocked softly, before it was opened by a servant inside.

Mangala gestured to them to go in, and stood with his back against the door.

The children entered a large square room with arched windows along one side, overlooking a grassy courtyard fringed with anthuriums. An open-fronted cabinet stood opposite, filled with brassy ornaments.

And there, standing in front of it, was the soon-to-be ruler of their island.

Chaya gawped, and heard the sharp intake of breath from Nour next to her.

Where the King was tall and muscular and brown, Sena was lightly built, slim and darker skinned. But that wasn't the only thing.

Serendib's new monarch wasn't the King's half-brother at all.

It was the King's half-sister.

Chapter
Thirty-Five

"Thank you for coming to see me," said Sena.

"You – you're welcome," said Chaya. For once she was speechless.

"I've been hearing about your exploits ever since the jewel theft." Sena laughed, and her tiny bell-like earrings shook. She wore cowled trousers and a fitted bodice, and her voice sounded vaguely foreign. As if reading Chaya's mind she said, "I've been away a long time, ever since my brother the King sent us away."

Of course. The King had banished both

his half-brother and half-sister.

"The real Sena died a long time ago." Her tone was full of pain, as if she hadn't got over it in all those years. "Ever since, I vowed to come back and take the throne and free this country from my tyrant brother. My journey back nearly took my life, but I'm here now and ready to serve Serendib."

Ready to serve Serendib. She sounded completely unlike the King.

She laughed again and looked at the three of them one by one. "Is anybody going to speak to me?"

"Sorry, Your Highness," said Neel. "What should we call you?"

"My name is Princess Leela. I know it's a lot to take in," she said. "I didn't set out to deceive anyone. I took on my brother's name and identity for my own safety as we travelled, and many people here don't know that he's gone yet. They assume it's he who is back for the throne."

Chaya nodded. As did she.

"Chaya, is it?" said the Princess. "Is your father the arrested headman?"

"Yes, he needs our help. All of our village does."

"I understand. I'm so sorry this has happened to you. I'll do everything I can to put things right."

"Thank you. We should act fast. The people are suffering."

Leela nodded and turned to Neel.

"Can I ask you something, Neelan? I'm not judging you and you don't have to answer if you don't want to, I'm just trying to understand this. Why did you steal the jewels?"

"I, er—"

"He didn't." Chaya stood very straight. "*I* am the jewel thief."

Leela didn't miss a beat. "Same question to you then."

"Someone I know, a boy my age, got attacked by a crocodile and needed to have some specialist treatment with a medicine man in Galle. His family needed to urgently come up with the money or he'd have lost his leg completely. One of his brothers even works at the palace, but there was no help for them."

"I see. That doesn't seem fair, does it?" Leela seemed to be absorbed in her thoughts for a bit, before she looked at them again. "We weren't ready for this so soon. We need to gather more supporters, consolidate our position further. But you're right, this is the best time to strike. And, more importantly, this is the time the people need it the most."

"The people of Nirissa would listen to us," said Chaya. "We can get them on your side. And if you bring your people, we could take on the King together."

"You're getting ahead of yourselves, children," said Mangala, speaking for the first time from his position at the back of the room. "It's not as easy as you think."

"I agree with Mangala," said Leela. "I won't jeopardise the safety of my troops by leading them on a foolish errand. We have no idea if your villagers will be receptive to you after all that's happened."

Chaya's heart sank. "Of course they will! They're our people."

"We will do our best to convince them, Princess Leela," said Neel. "You can count on us."

"I know I can," said Leela. "That's why I think you should go to your village and try to get your people on our side. But I'm not risking the lives of my army by taking them there when I don't know what your villagers' reaction would be. They might still side with the King."

"That's right." Mangala nodded in approval. "The Princess is right to cover all bases. Your safety is important, Leela. It'll be up to you kids to go and meet your people, of course."

"Oh no, you've got that completely wrong, Mangala," said Leela. "I won't risk my troops marching in there. I'll be going to Nirissa with the children myself."

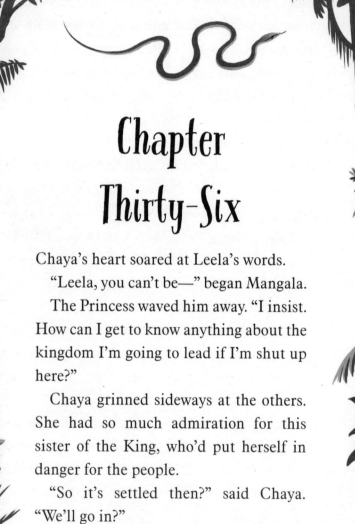

Chapter
Thirty-Six

Chaya's heart soared at Leela's words.

"Leela, you can't be—" began Mangala.

The Princess waved him away. "I insist.
How can I get to know anything about the
kingdom I'm going to lead if I'm shut up
here?"

Chaya grinned sideways at the others.
She had so much admiration for this
sister of the King, who'd put herself in
danger for the people.

"So it's settled then?" said Chaya.
"We'll go in?"

"We will," said Leela. "Our task is to

meet your people and get them onside. We can take a couple of Gamage's men with us. My supporters, led by my own General, will amass in the jungle, close to Nirissa, ready to attack. As soon as we give the signal that all is ready, they'll come in. We need the villagers to be prepared and willing, with whatever weapons they have."

Nour had gone white. Leela noticed.

"You have one task," said Leela. "And only one. All you need to do is help get your people on board, and have them join us against the King. Without that my people can't advance, *and they won't advance*. Because I need to think about everyone else I'm bringing in too."

"Of course," said Chaya.

"Once you've done that," Leela looked quite serious, "I need you three out of the way. I can't emphasise that enough. It'll make me very angry if you don't heed this."

Chaya looked away. Go back to the village and hide like cowards while people fight for their lives? She didn't know about Neel and Nour, but if Leela thought she was going to listen to *that* she was very much mistaken.

Chapter Thirty-Seven

The next day dawned dark and gloomy. The air was swollen with dampness, and clouds hung low in the sky.

"Do you think this could be the King's last day as king?" said Chaya, surveying the sky through the barred window. They were back at Gamage's hideout, and would be joined by Leela to go to Nirissa.

Nour was looking pale and drawn. "I don't know how you're so calm."

"We have each other," said Neel. "And Ananda. We're taking him, did you know that?"

Chaya turned back to the room. "It makes sense, I suppose. We're going to be walking the whole day. Once the village is dark and asleep we'll sneak in."

"Why does it have to be dark?" said Nour.

"The village is full of the King's men by day. Once they've left for the night is the best time to get in. If we're caught before we can speak to our people and explain things that'll be terrible."

Neel nodded thoughtfully. "We need to get to them before the King gets to us."

Nour drew her feet up and wrapped her arms around her legs, her feet peeping out from under her now-clean skirt. "I wish I could be like you two. I'll be less than useless."

"You'll be fine," said Chaya, looking through the window at one of the men coming towards their hut. "We just need to be on our toes."

The door swung inwards. "Gamage wants you now," said the man, gesturing to them to come with him. "I'm Rameez. I'll be coming with you too."

They followed him down the coconut-husk-strewn path to the platform, where all the bandits sat crowded around Gamage.

They almost didn't recognise Leela when they saw her. She was dressed like a villager, in a frayed blouse and shabby skirt that trailed the ground. Chaya watched the men closely. Did they realise that the future Queen of Serendib was in their midst?

Chaya, Neel and Nour huddled together, with the three adults leading the way. Ananda walked beside them, a bag of supplies on his back. Gamage kept a respectful distance from Leela, nodding eagerly at whatever she said. He was obviously in on the secret.

"A whole day of walking," said Nour. "At least we're going back home. Gamage knows the jungle so well, we'll be there in no time."

They continued as before, passing through all manner of jungle. Darkness was falling and Rameez took out a metal pitcher from the bag on Ananda's side and began to drum on it loudly.

"*What* is he doing?" said Nour.

"Oh, it's just to warn animals that humans are about."

Night was near, and birds twittered and cricket sounds pierced the air.

Chaya began to think of tactics. "Since Father is in jail there's no point going to my part of the village. And no point going to the City either. The rich people aren't going to join in the uprising."

Neel nodded. "We can meet lots of people quickly

if we go round my way. They're the people who have suffered the most too."

That made sense, going to Neel's part of the village. Clusters of little houses crowded between clumps of greenery. It was where the King's men went that very first time after Chaya stole the jewels, where she'd seen the men throw the contents of houses on to the ground outside.

Rameez had stopped his drumming, and they rustled quietly onwards.

Leela and the men were waiting for them to catch up at the very edge of the jungle. Everyone bunched around in the near darkness.

"This is where we stop and wait." Leela spoke softly, even though they couldn't possibly be overheard by anyone here. "We'll go in as soon as we're sure the King's men have retreated. The village probably will be asleep too. We'll leave Ananda here. It'll be quieter without him now!"

"What about your army?" said Chaya.

"There's an ancient temple in the middle of the jungle where they're assembling. Once they have our signal they can get here in two hours. The villagers have time to be ready and waiting then."

Nour was breathing hard next to Chaya. Even in

the half-darkness Chaya could see Neel's face was pale. She took both their hands in hers and squeezed. "It's time."

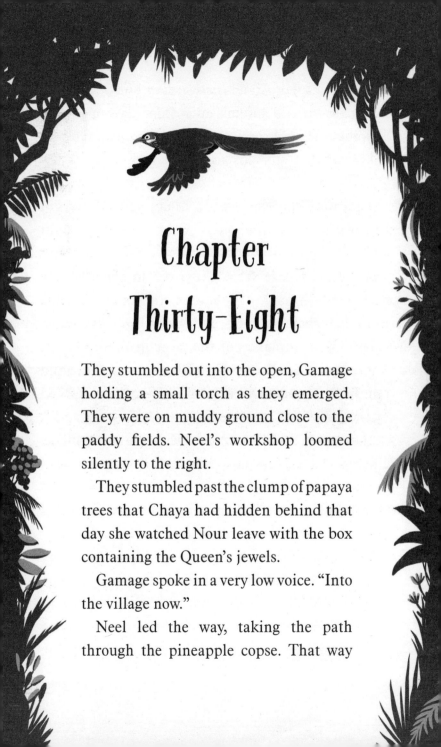

Chapter Thirty-Eight

They stumbled out into the open, Gamage holding a small torch as they emerged. They were on muddy ground close to the paddy fields. Neel's workshop loomed silently to the right.

They stumbled past the clump of papaya trees that Chaya had hidden behind that day she watched Nour leave with the box containing the Queen's jewels.

Gamage spoke in a very low voice. "Into the village now."

Neel led the way, taking the path through the pineapple copse. That way they avoided Jamis and his warning horn, which he used to scare wild animals away from his crops.

Spiky pineapple crowns scratched against Chaya's ankles as they walked, and Nour suppressed a few gasps.

They were approaching the village now, the rows of tiny wattle and daub houses squatting to their right and left in front of them.

A gentle breeze from the river in the distance whispered through the houses, lifting up strands from their thatched roofs, and then all was still again. Chaya tried to make out the river in the darkness. There was a gentle lap-lap of water, and she could faintly see the muddy bank where Vijay was attacked by the crocodile.

"Let's go to Siva," said Neel. "He's one of the village elders so we can speak to him first and then spread the word from there."

"Yes," said Chaya. Siva was reasonable, she liked him. "It's that house there."

She followed Gamage, Rameez and Leela, and they tiptoed towards the line of houses. *This one?* Gamage mouthed, holding up his torch at the door.

The flame of his torch caught the thatch, and a spark licked its way across the roof. Gamage swore and flapped at it with his other hand, trying to put out the fire.

Chaya started and the scream died in her throat.

The flames flared right up and in a moment caught the roof of the next house too.

Chapter Thirty-Nine

"No!" Chaya screamed, and tried to get to the door, but Neel pushed her aside and hammered on it.

Within minutes people had woken and came running from the surrounding houses.

A woman with a baby came coughing and sputtering towards them, and grabbed Chaya. "You! It's you who's done this. Look who's back," she yelled.

"Wait, no," said Chaya, pulling herself away. "We came to help."

"We need to get out of here," Gamage

said urgently. "Come on."

"No!" cried Chaya. "We need to help put this out."

"We're not going anywhere," said Neel.

"Princess," Gamage whispered. "We must leave."

But Leela disregarded him completely. "Get him out," she yelled at a man who was bent over a slumbering figure inside the house. "Bring him into the fresh air."

"Please, Princess Leela," said Gamage. "Come on!"

"Nobody knows who I am," said Leela, before darting in to help the man.

More doors were knocked down and people pulled out. A boy with a very singed shirt emerged, limping.

"Wait a minute," said the woman to Gamage and Rameez. "Who are you? I think I know you!"

At that Rameez melted away into the darkness.

"Bandits! You're with the bandits!" screamed the woman.

"They are trying to help you," said Nour.

"We don't need your help!" She spat at the ground. "How dare you come back here after all the trouble you've caused."

A few other villagers surrounded Chaya, Neel and Leela. Nour stayed on the periphery.

"Listen," said Neel, speaking fast. "Hear us out.

The fire was an accident. We came to help you. We know what the King did, and you don't have to put up with it any more. We have people who will fight for you."

A look of pure terror flashed across the woman's face. "No! Don't you dare speak like that. We're in enough trouble as it is. We don't want you making things worse."

"Please, you don't have to be afraid of the King any more," said Neel, but a man hit him across the face and grabbed him roughly.

"Stop that!" yelled Leela. "You're wasting time! We need help here. The fire is spreading further."

"We've had enough of you lot and your trickery," the man said. "We're not listening to a word you say. You're all going to the King."

Chaya stared at Neel in horror. The people were siding with the King!

"They were with bandits!" said the woman with the baby. "Led them here to rob us all!"

"No, it isn't like that!" said Chaya. But no one was listening. They'd got it all wrong. From the corner of her eye she saw Nour slip away.

"Never mind about the King or the bandits," said Leela. "I tell you, we need help here. The villagers can't control this."

The fire roared and caught a clump of trees, and that in turn caught another row of houses.

People screamed and backed away, but Chaya's captors kept a hold of her.

"It's spreading!" shouted someone. The woman with the baby screamed and ran towards the fire. Still Chaya was in someone's grip, unable to get free.

"Let me go," said Neel, trying to get free of his captors. "It's going towards my house. LET ME GO."

"We need help!" said Chaya, still struggling. Leela was right, the villagers were struggling to contain the fire. She aimed a kick at one of them. "Let me go."

The villagers were out of their depth. Some were trying to break down a door, others were organising buckets. The fire kept spreading, the wind taking it to more houses.

"Stop it!" yelled Chaya. She hit out at one of the men and caught him in the jaw, but he grabbed her and pinned her hands behind her back.

The fire flared high and crackled into the sky. Neel stared at it, inching towards his house. Suddenly he stiffened and turned to Chaya.

There was an expression she couldn't read flickering on his face. *What*, she mouthed.

He was trying to tell her something.

There came a trumpeting.

Ananda!

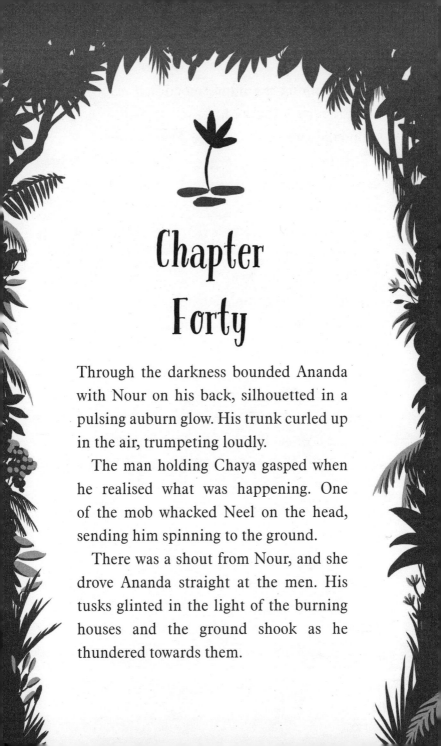

Chapter Forty

Through the darkness bounded Ananda with Nour on his back, silhouetted in a pulsing auburn glow. His trunk curled up in the air, trumpeting loudly.

The man holding Chaya gasped when he realised what was happening. One of the mob whacked Neel on the head, sending him spinning to the ground.

There was a shout from Nour, and she drove Ananda straight at the men. His tusks glinted in the light of the burning houses and the ground shook as he thundered towards them.

In a moment the mob's mood had changed from anger to terror. Even Chaya felt a thrill of horror as Ananda's powerful body bore down on them.

The men scattered in panic. "Come on," shouted Nour, Ananda's trumpeting booming through the smoke.

Chaya sprinted towards her, but Neel darted away to his home.

"We need the King's men at once. The fire's spreading." Chaya hoisted herself on Ananda and urged him on. "This way, Ananda."

"They're going to catch us," said Nour. "Shouldn't we get away?"

"We can't. We need the King's men." She shouted a warning to Leela: "The King's men will be here soon."

Ananda drew back and shook his head at the smoke drifting from the village. But Chaya rubbed her foot on his right ear and turned him left, skirting the village as she made for the High Road. Lines of flames snaked through the village and a couple of roofs blazed in waves of scarlet fire.

Close to the walls of the city she made straight for the old war bell. "*Stop*, Ananda."

Chaya manoeuvred Ananda over the crumbling plinth and patted him to calm him as the smoke drifted up and made Chaya cough. "Stay still, Ananda. Trust me. Be good now."

She bent down and rubbed his head. "There's going to be noise." Ananda carried the King at the head of all the pageants; he was well used to the sounds of crowds and fireworks and mayhem. But she had to warn him anyway. "Cover your ears," she yelled at Nour.

Chaya pulled herself up to a standing position, swaying and holding out her arms to get her balance as her feet rested on Ananda's warm back. She lifted the clapper and sent it crashing down with all her strength. Thrusting her hands over her ears she flopped down on Ananda and they drove him away as the deafening sounds tore through the air, the peals echoing all around the villages and into the night sky.

Chapter Forty-One

Chaya led Ananda back to the village. Nour pulled her tattered shawl over her nose and mouth as they made their way.

"Neel will be with his family," said Nour. "I hope they're safe."

Chaya hoped so too. Her own home wasn't anywhere close to the fire, and Nour's family were in the city so would be safe.

They left Ananda near the river. "*Stay*, Ananda. You'll be safe here."

The village was in uproar. People screamed and ran about, looking to see if loved ones were safe. Water sloshed as a line of villagers passed buckets from the well. A man ran around asking people if they'd seen his child.

To their surprise Leela was still there, comforting a woman who had a burn on her leg. The first of the King's men had started filtering through, taking control of things at once.

"Here she is again!" shouted the woman with the baby. "Thought you could run away, did you?"

"We weren't running away," said Chaya. Nour edged close to her. "I told you, we're trying to help you."

"Help us? How?" The woman advanced, her baby clutched to her chest. Onlookers drew nearer, forming a circle around them.

Chaya lowered her voice. "We can work together against the King. We don't have to live like this, in fear all the time. The King's half-sister is ready to fight him and take the throne, with our support."

The people stared at her with hostility in their eyes. It was as if they didn't even know her. Bala's parents, Kumar the carpenter, a farmer Chaya'd helped once, friends of Father's.

"Don't even start with your lies," said the woman with the baby. "We're not going to let you drag us into any of your schemes and suffer any more than we already have, thanks to you. You're nothing but a liar and a thief, and now you've gone and joined another set of thieves." She spat on the ground. "And you want to put us in even more danger."

"Is anyone hurt?" asked Chaya.

"They're fine, no thanks to you!" said a man with a singed shirt. "But someone could have been."

There was a scuffle in the crowd as Neel pushed his way to the middle. "They did nothing, let them go!"

"Look!" Someone in the crowd pointed. "That's Neelan, the jewel thief."

"He's not the jewel thief. I am!"

"You're both as bad as each other. And dragging *her* with you. What did you want, a ransom from the merchant?"

"You've got it all wrong," said Chaya.

"I always knew you were a bad one," said another man. "Your poor late mother must be squirming in her ashes."

The fire was dying down, now that the King's men were bringing it under control.

"Guards," shouted the woman with the baby. "Here, take them."

Chaya's heart began to beat in her ears. "No, really.

We weren't going to rob you. We came here to help you."

"It's the truth," said Neel. "We would never hurt any of you."

"Liars!" The woman shook her fist at them. "My children could have been killed in their sleep."

A group of the King's men came forward and one of the villagers indicated Chaya and Neel. "They did this."

"This is the jewel thief," said an older woman, thumping Neel on the back. "I found him for the King."

"Not just the jewel thief," said the woman with the baby. "The girl who got him out of jail. And not only that, but then they go and join that lot in the jungle and bring them here."

The leader of the group of King's men, an older man, raised his eyebrows. "They were with bandits?"

"Yes, they came here to loot and burn our houses."

Chaya felt sick. This was it then.

The crowd was turning to their right, everyone craning to look at something coming towards them. Over their heads Chaya saw Ananda, being led by a boy. "It's the King's elephant! They'd left him by the river."

The older guard turned back to them and sighed. "Let's see now. Stealing the Queen's jewels; breaking into jail and releasing all the prisoners; causing damage and destruction in the royal compound; stealing the King's elephant; bringing bandits into the village and finally setting fire to it." He tutted under his breath. "You can kiss your lives goodbye."

Chaya felt numb. Next to her she felt Nour shiver.

"I tell you it was me," said Neel. "I made them do all of it."

"Oh, shut up," said the guard. "You three are more trouble than it's worth."

"Five," shouted a man, pointing at Leela and Gamage. "Don't forget the bandits."

A shadow passed over Leela's face.

The guard shouted out an order. "Men. Round them all up. We're taking them to the King."

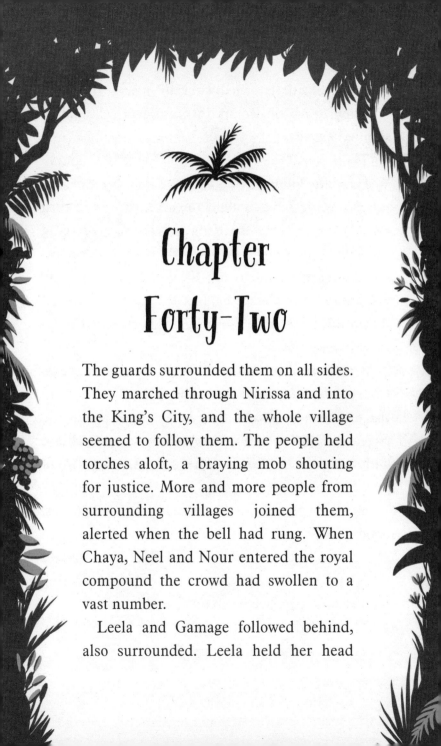

Chapter Forty-Two

The guards surrounded them on all sides. They marched through Nirissa and into the King's City, and the whole village seemed to follow them. The people held torches aloft, a braying mob shouting for justice. More and more people from surrounding villages joined them, alerted when the bell had rung. When Chaya, Neel and Nour entered the royal compound the crowd had swollen to a vast number.

Leela and Gamage followed behind, also surrounded. Leela held her head high, walking determinedly ahead.

"They nearly killed us in our sleep," the crowd shouted angrily.

"*The traitors*."

"Hang the lot of them!"

Who would have thought the villagers would turn against them? Once the King saw them, everything would be over. They'd been caught with the Princess – the biggest threat to the King's reign. Her army wouldn't have a chance against the King's men even if they advanced now. The villagers had made sure of that.

As they were jostled in through the palace gates, Chaya looked behind her. The villagers filled up the promenade, just as they had a week ago at the pageant. The lion statue towered above them, ablaze with two giant torches on either side. A lone figure in purple stood there, watching. General Siri.

They were pushed up the stairs by a band of guards. Nour clutched at Chaya's hand. She was drenched in sweat, and Neel looked pale and ill. Chaya gasped when she saw the crowds below – a sea of floating torches on the palace promenade and lawns.

"The crowd must stay there," said General Siri. "Let only the children through."

The guards beat back the throng trying to follow up the stairs.

"Back! Only the prisoners from this point!"

General Siri considered them as they went up. "Who's the girl in the middle?"

"She's the daughter of the merchant, Cassim," said Chaya. "She's completely innocent."

"I didn't ask for your opinion." He pointed at Nour. "How did you get mixed up with them?"

Nour looked petrified. "I – I … I don't know."

Neel stopped near General Siri too. "Chaya didn't do anything either, sir. It was all me. I forced her to do everything she did. Please let her go."

Lovely, loyal Neel. The idea that he could force her to do anything!

General Siri smirked, his bottom lip quivering like a leech. "You're in no position to ask for anything. Take them inside. And who are these?"

He was pointing at Gamage and Leela.

"Bandits, General," said a guard. "The children brought them to the village."

Leela stared straight at General Siri, but he hardly gave her a second look. He waved them away, saying, "Throw them into the dungeons too."

They all trudged past General Siri and into the

inner palace complex. Tiny torches twinkled all over the dark courtyard, the amber flames reflected in the rectangular pools on either side.

"Where are you taking us?" Chaya asked a guard.

"You heard the General. To the dungeons for the night. The King will see you in the morning."

Neel gasped. "The King himself?"

"Have you seen the crowd outside? This has become so big he'll hear you out in person." He shrugged. "I reckon it's certain death."

Neel dropped his voice. "Listen, Chaya, they think I stole the jewels. I'm going to admit to everything else. I don't want you to complicate anything by butting in."

"What kind of a useless friend do you think I am? Sorry, I can't let you do that."

"Please, Chaya, listen to me. Leela's been caught. Everything is over. At least you and Nour can escape with your lives."

"No," said Chaya. "Never."

"You have so much going for you. I'm just a poor woodworker. As long as my parents are provided for no one is going to miss me."

Tears were falling freely on Nour's cheeks as she listened.

"That's not true," said Chaya. "And you know it."

"Chaya, please."

Chaya tried to stop the sob that was threatening to escape. "When have I ever listened to you, Neel? I'm not about to start now."

Neel looked at her sadly. "I'm sorry. For everything."

Light and shadow criss-crossed the blue-tinged stone walls as they went through to the dungeons. And far below them the crowds waited.

The guards fanned out all over the place. There would be no escaping now.

They were finally at the mercy of the King.

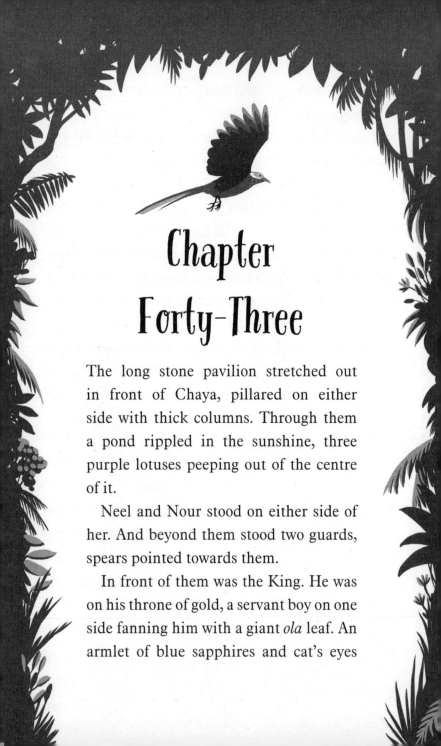

Chapter Forty-Three

The long stone pavilion stretched out in front of Chaya, pillared on either side with thick columns. Through them a pond rippled in the sunshine, three purple lotuses peeping out of the centre of it.

Neel and Nour stood on either side of her. And beyond them stood two guards, spears pointed towards them.

In front of them was the King. He was on his throne of gold, a servant boy on one side fanning him with a giant *ola* leaf. An armlet of blue sapphires and cat's eyes encircled the King's muscular upper arm, the jewels bigger than any Chaya had seen. He leaned forward and looked down at her. He wore his hair tied up in a knot on his head, ringed with a band of gold.

He couldn't look more different from Leela.

Leela, who was imprisoned at the moment in the King's dungeons.

One of the guards holding the spear looked at Chaya from the corner of his eye. He was very young and there was something vaguely familiar about him.

"So." The King's hooded gaze travelled over Chaya, Nour and Neel. "Am I to believe that these are the cause of so much chaos in my kingdom?" He leaned back on his throne. "Three *children*?"

"That's right, Your Majesty," said General Siri from where he was standing on the left of the throne. Alongside him sat a row of important people in gilt armchairs – lords of the different provinces of Serendib. "The boy has just turned thirteen – hardly a child."

Chaya glared at the General. As if that made any difference.

"And the girls outwitted a whole battalion of guards to release him from prison?"

General Siri went red. "It appears so. The girl in the centre is a cunning, devious child who's caused no end of trouble for her village."

"I see," said the King. "So this is her. The girl who stole an elephant."

"That's right, Your Majesty," said General Siri. "She's the daughter of the headman of Nirissa."

"Ah," said the King. "The man who claims to know nothing about anything."

"That's because he doesn't," said Chaya. "He hasn't heard a word from me since I left."

General Siri silenced her with a look. "They had help as well. Two bandits they led into the village were captured with them."

"Good," said the King. "They'll have the same punishment."

"May I speak, Your Majesty?" came a voice from the back. Chaya turned to see Aunty, along with the rest of the villagers of Nirissa, who had been given special dispensation to stay and watch.

The King waved a hand at her.

"My niece," she said, her voice breaking. "Please, Your Majesty. She's been very foolish. But she's just a child. Please forgive her. I'll make sure she is punished and will never do such a thing again. I will take her away, far away from here so she doesn't cause any more trouble."

"I don't think so," said the King. He rested his arms on the sides of his seat. "She must answer for her crimes."

"Your M—" began Aunty.

"Silence!" said General Siri. "Don't answer back to His Majesty if you know what's good for you. This isn't only about the jewels. People would have *died* yesterday if we didn't get to the village when we did."

"Who's the other girl?" The King clicked his fingers at the servant boy to fan faster.

"A curious story," said General Siri. "When Her Majesty the Queen got her jewels back she noticed something strange. The jewels were in an expensive drawstring bag, the type of material of which is not to be found in this island."

Chaya's heart sank. She'd put the jewels in her pouch when she stole them, until she packed them into Neel's box. But when Nour brought them back it was definitely in a drawstring bag, all transparent geometric silk with a pretty ribbon.

General Siri cleared his throat. "Perhaps the cinnamon peeler's son had a spare one lying around his house? Or Headman Sarath collected his wages for a year and got one of the silk merchants to bring one back from his next trip? Can *someone* explain?"

Chapter
Forty-Four

Chaya gulped. Poor Nour. She had nothing to do with the robbery. Although it was telling that the Queen hadn't even noticed the missing cat's eye pendant that had paid for Vijay's treatment.

"I – it's mine," said Nour. "The bag was mine. But I didn't steal the jewels."

The King looked furious. "Why would the jewels be in your bag then?"

"I didn't, Your Majesty." Nour took a deep breath. "It's a long story. But the jewels were put into a wooden box in Neelan's carpentry workshop, then

I bought the box and took it home. Then I put the jewels into this bag and left the box on my dressing table. And then Chaya stole the box from *me*. Then I went back to the workshop with the jewels in the—"

"ENOUGH," shouted the King. He stood up in a rage, spitting out his words and his eyes bulging from their sockets. "Do you take me for a fool?"

Everyone shrank back at the King's outburst, except General Siri, who didn't even flinch.

"It's the truth," said Chaya. "Ask her father. Or the carpenter, Kumar. They were both there when Nour bought the box."

"The merchant Cassim is out of town," said General Siri. "Looking for his daughter. As he has been since she went missing.

"In any case, I recall seeing both girls at the carpenter's workshop when the boy was arrested." He turned to the King. "The girl denies the charge. Even though the evidence is clear that she's involved."

"I sentence her to death," said the King.

"You can't do this!" said Chaya. "Nour is innocent."

"Please, Your Majesty—" started Neel.

"Keep quiet, both of you," snapped General Siri. "Don't speak out of turn to the King."

"But she's innocent. She did noth—"

"I told you to shut up."

General Siri unrolled a document and read from it. "You, Neelan, son of Ram the cinnamon peeler, do you admit to breaking into the palace and stealing the Queen's jewels?"

"Yes, sir. All on my own."

"Do you admit to leading two criminals into Nirissa village with the intent to damage and loot?"

"Yes, sir."

General Siri folded up the document.

"I sentence the boy to death," said the King.

A fire danced deep in Chaya's chest. The King had made his decision so quickly, without an ounce of feeling. A cry came from somewhere. Neel's mother was sobbing from the back, in the crowd of villagers along with Aunty.

"You, Chaya, daughter of Headman Sarath," said General Siri, reading from a different document. "Do you admit to helping Neelan, son of Ram, escape prison?"

"Yes, but only because he shouldn't have been—"

"I told you to *shut up*. Just answer the question. Do you admit to leading two criminals into Nirissa village with the intent to rob and destroy?"

Chaya gulped. "The fire was an accident—"

"Do you admit to stealing the King's elephant?"

"That, yes. Totally."

General Siri looked at the King. "The girl has admitted to all charges against her too."

"No, I—"

The King's voice rasped out his verdict. "The girl dies too."

On Chaya's left the guard with the spear sighed and closed his eyes.

The King flicked his hand. "Get them out of my sight, and do it *now*."

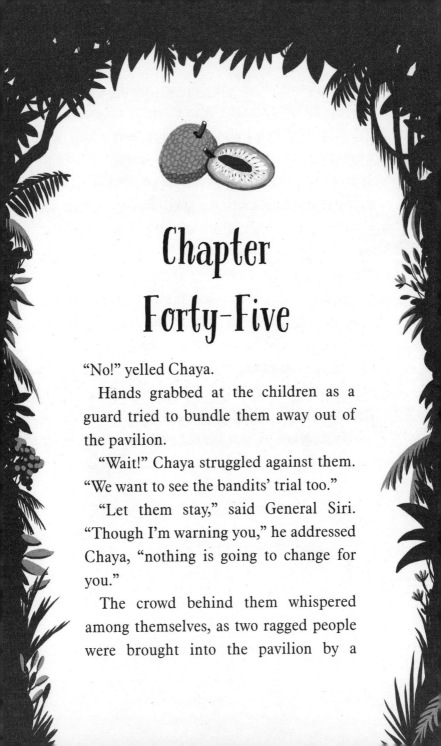

Chapter Forty-Five

"No!" yelled Chaya.

Hands grabbed at the children as a guard tried to bundle them away out of the pavilion.

"Wait!" Chaya struggled against them. "We want to see the bandits' trial too."

"Let them stay," said General Siri. "Though I'm warning you," he addressed Chaya, "nothing is going to change for you."

The crowd behind them whispered among themselves, as two ragged people were brought into the pavilion by a cluster of guards. They weren't putting up a struggle, but walked freely towards the King. It was Gamage and Leela. Her head was held high as always, and her eyes were fixed on the King as she came up the wide stone steps. In spite of her raggedness there was something majestic about her small figure, making its way surely towards the front of the pavilion and the King.

The King hardly looked at them. "Get this over with quickly," he said to General Siri.

Gamage stopped to the left of the trio, but Leela walked on, to stand just in front of the King.

"What are you doing?" yelled General Siri. "Stand back from the King."

The King looked up in surprise.

"Hello, brother." Leela smiled up at him. "It's been a long time."

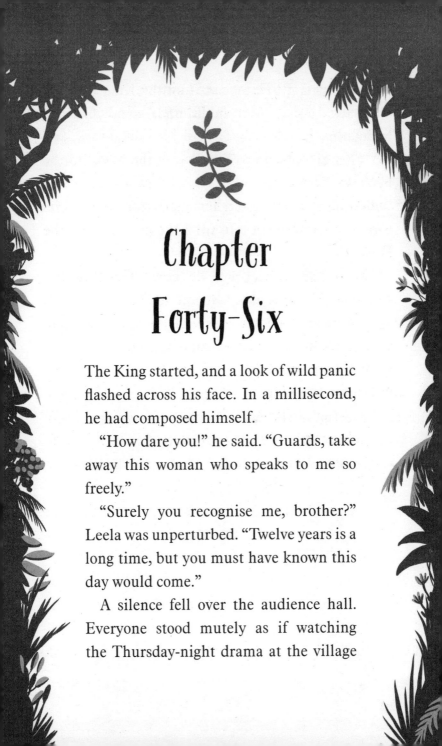

Chapter
Forty-Six

The King started, and a look of wild panic flashed across his face. In a millisecond, he had composed himself.

"How dare you!" he said. "Guards, take away this woman who speaks to me so freely."

"Surely you recognise me, brother?" Leela was unperturbed. "Twelve years is a long time, but you must have known this day would come."

A silence fell over the audience hall. Everyone stood mutely as if watching the Thursday-night drama at the village square. General Siri looked from the King to Leela and back again, as if trying to understand what was happening.

"What are you doing?" bellowed the King. "Seize her, *now*! Both of them."

The King's outburst galvanised the guards into action. They jumped forward but Leela held up her hand.

"There's no need for that. I'll come quietly. But you need to listen to me first." She turned to the crowd. "I am the King's half-sister, daughter of your old King. I came back, not to cause trouble, but to help my people."

Behind them the villagers looked astounded. *Princess Leela?* Her name rippled through the crowd, incredulously at first. Then, reverently.

"They don't need your help!" shouted the King.

Leela was unruffled. "That is not for you to say."

"Do you," General Siri sputtered, "do you want them taken away now, Your Majesty?"

"Be quiet, General," said Leela. "I won't be long." She addressed the people again. "We don't have to live like this. In fear all the time, with everyone only fending for themselves. I'm here for you."

"You!" The King laughed mirthlessly. "You think

the people are going to listen to you? They know that what's good for them is a strong leader who will rule with an iron fist. Not you. *They* will never accept *you*."

"There is no they or me, brother. There is only us."

The villagers muttered among themselves. They seemed unsure and scared.

"What are you waiting for!" The King paced to the end of his platform and yelled at General Siri. "Take them away. All of them! Put them to death at once. And anyone who's caught agreeing with a word this crazy woman has said," he glared at the people threateningly, "will be dead too."

Chapter Forty-Seven

The children were hauled out first.

"Good riddance," whispered a villager as they were dragged past. "Our troubles will be over at last with you gone."

"You don't have to do this!" yelled Chaya. "Why do we have to be ruled by someone everyone is scared of? We can put this right together."

"Keep quiet, *thief*," said a woman. "Don't make the King angrier than he is already."

"Neelan," wailed his mother, and she tried to clutch him as they dragged him past.

"We were only going to help you." Nour's face was streaked with tears.

"Why do you think Chaya rang the bell?" said Neel. "That brought the King's men and they put out the fire. We could have run away but she saved the village instead."

A couple of the villagers looked confused, and chattered among each other. "That couldn't have been her," said one. "The plinth is broken – she couldn't reach the bell."

"She stood on the elephant," said Nour. "Think about it; no one else could have rung it."

"We don't believe you liars," said the woman with the baby from earlier. "Steal is all she's ever done. Don't think we don't know, just because she hasn't been caught before."

"And now she's trying to be a revolutionary." An old man cackled and people around him joined in.

"Yes, I'm a thief!" Chaya yelled with all her might, for all her taunters to hear. "But you know what, my thieving paid for your roof, Chathura."

Chathura looked startled, and there was an "Is that true?" from someone close to him. He nodded slowly.

"And you, Sumana." Chaya jabbed her finger at the people she'd helped as a guard pushed her roughly through the crowd. "My thieving paid for your son's books, and Vijay's leg and David's vegetable cart."

Murmurs ran through the crowd.

"And Tuan would be dead, and Marikkar's children starved if it wasn't for my thieving!"

People were starting to look uncomfortable now.

"And you say you're a strong leader, brother." Leela's voice rang out and a hush fell over everyone. "A child needs to steal so that the basic needs of your people are met."

The guard pointing his spear at Leela looked at Chaya across the crowds. His familiar face creased into a look of resolve. He drew back the spear and rested it on the ground.

"What are you doing?" yelled the King.

The guard stared at the King obstinately, then dropped the spear on the floor, where it fell with a clatter.

"Well done, son," shouted a female voice from the back.

And that's when Chaya realised why he looked so familiar. The guard was Vijay's brother, the boy she'd stolen the jewels for.

Seeing this, the guard next to Gamage lowered his spear too.

"She's right," shouted one of the villagers. "Why *should* we live like this?"

"While the King and his ministers grow richer on our country's wealth," shouted someone else.

The lords of Serendib's provinces looked on stonily.

For the first time, a look of fear crossed the King's face.

The hands binding Chaya dropped away. Leela took a step forward.

General Siri watched and said nothing, waiting to see which side to choose.

The villagers advanced to the front of the pavilion, filtering through the guards, who put down their weapons.

From beyond the pavilion came more villagers, until clusters of them were amassed round the pavilion.

You could hear a pin drop.

There was no need for an attack. The King and his few supporters were well and truly outnumbered.

Leela advanced, until she was standing at the foot of the throne.

The King gulped. "Very well," he said.

General Siri's voice rang out over everyone as the King stepped down.

"All hail the new Queen of Serendib!"

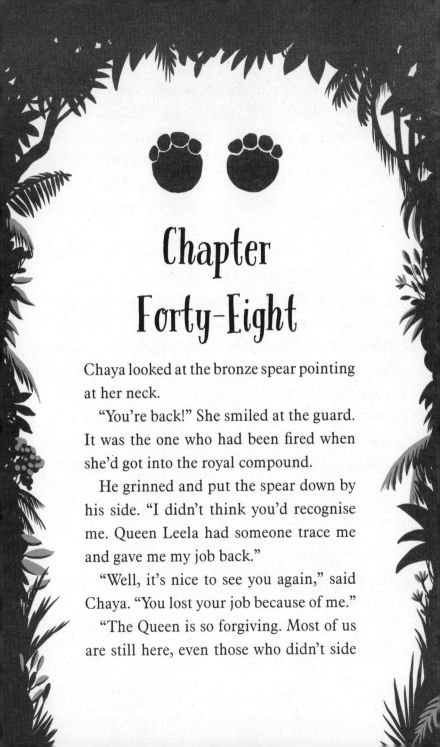

Chapter
Forty-Eight

Chaya looked at the bronze spear pointing at her neck.

"You're back!" She smiled at the guard. It was the one who had been fired when she'd got into the royal compound.

He grinned and put the spear down by his side. "I didn't think you'd recognise me. Queen Leela had someone trace me and gave me my job back."

"Well, it's nice to see you again," said Chaya. "You lost your job because of me."

"The Queen is so forgiving. Most of us are still here, even those who didn't side with her to begin with. By the way, I'm not going to let you go up there today. *Anything past the lion's entrance is strictly out of bounds to the public*, remember?"

"I'm actually here by invitation," said Chaya grandly. She pulled out a rolled-up card and gave it to him. It was a request to go and see General Siri for a special reward.

He read it and whistled. "All right, go on up. Someone will direct you to General Siri's offices."

Neel was already waiting when she was shown in, and Nour came in shortly after. A guard then pointed them into a large room with a wide window overlooking the promenade.

General Siri leaned on the edge of an ornate ebony desk, waiting for them. He seemed to have been relegated to a clerical position, but in spite of that everything about the room was dazzlingly rich, from the creamy velvet seats of the heavily carved chairs to the jewel-studded letter opener on the table.

"Leave us," he said to the guard.

Through the window behind him they could see families milling about in the grounds, enjoying a feast being held to mark the beginning of a new reign.

"The Queen has requested I give you these," said General Siri, handing over three silver plaques. He couldn't have looked more miserable if he tried. "They award you the status of Heroes of Serendib. There will be a ceremony at a later date, after her coronation."

"Thank you," said Chaya. "Although you don't look too thrilled about it."

Neel kicked Chaya with the side of his foot.

General Siri's face hardened. He walked up to the window and looked out at the crowds. "Don't get cocky, child. You can leave now."

When they came back down to the promenade Aunty was waiting with Father. She hugged Chaya until her breath was almost squeezed out of her. "Hero of Serendib indeed!" She laughed. "As if your head could get any bigger than it already is."

Chaya laughed, then gestured towards Nour, who was standing slightly back. "Aunty, this is my friend, Nour."

Nour blushed.

"What a pretty girl," said Aunty. "Maybe you'll be a calming influence on Chaya."

Nour giggled. "Oh, I don't know about that."

"Don't count on it," said Father. "If Neelan couldn't do it in all this time I doubt anyone can."

"Father! I've changed. Honest."

"She hasn't," said Neel.

Father beamed proudly. "The King stood no chance against you three. It was nice that it was a peaceful coup, without a drop of blood being shed. And *almost* worth all the hassle you gave me."

"I'm so sorry for everything I put you through, Father," said Chaya. "I really am."

Father smiled. "I know you are. Whatever headaches you cause me, no one can doubt you do everything out of love."

"Look," said Chaya, embarrassed. "The sweetmeats are out."

The palace servants ran around like ants, managing the feast. There was dancing and singing, and soon the veenas burst into melody too.

"Come on," said Chaya, pulling Neel and Nour towards the sweetmeats stall.

Nour put some sweets on a plate. "I guess this is the end of your thieving days then."

"Why'd you think that?" said Chaya, biting into a syrupy dough ball. "Things are great and I'm sure the new Queen will look after the people who need it most. But who knows, if people need it, help is at hand."

"You are joking, aren't you?" said Neel.

Chaya licked the syrup off her fingers and slipped her hand into her pocket. Nour gasped and Neel slapped his hand on his forehead as Chaya twirled General Siri's letter opener in their faces.

"Relax," she said, pocketing it. "He has too much stuff to miss it. I'll put it to good use if someone is in need."

"Chaya," said Nour. "I will never understand you. But I have one question. When you broke into my house, why didn't you steal any of those sugary sweets that you love so much? When I gave them to you in the jungle that was the first time you'd tasted them."

Chaya smiled as she popped another dough ball in her mouth. "What do you think I am? A thief or something?"

She looked around her. Clusters of people stood chatting on the green, laughing with each other. Sweetmeats sizzled in hot oil, throwing their aroma around the lawns. Children darted through the crowds playing, and the three of them were back safe with their families at last. Serendib had a wise and just new Queen who would rule with care and love. And in the middle of it all Ananda lifted up his majestic head and trumpeted into the blue, blue sky.

Acknowledgements

Ananda-sized thanks go out to my editor, Kirsty Stansfield, for the care and attention given to this newbie author, and to Rebecca, Julia and everyone at Nosy Crow for your work on this book.

To my agent, Joanna Moult, thank you for your guidance, advice, and for championing me from the very beginning. You really are the sapphire that shines the bluest of blues.

To my designer, Nicola Theobald, and illustrator, David Dean, for bringing the world of my imagination to life so magnificently on the cover and insides.

Massive thanks and gratitude to Julia Green. I learnt more from you in a term than in my whole writing life, and this book is so much richer for it. Also to Steve Voake, my manuscript tutor, without whom my story would have been a much quieter one! To CJ Skuse and Janine Amos, for your help and encouragement in getting the characters and setting out of me.

Thank you to the (hopefully lifelong) friends I've made in the BSU gang. I don't know how I'd have done it without the lovely Aubergine group. In particular, much appreciation and lots of jambu to Yasmin Rahman, for the listening ear and the late night chats amidst much tension and ear flapping at every stage. I also value the occasional nugget of wisdom you quite accidentally dispense. To Hana Tooke, for your structural insights, always showing me the way when I can't see the jungle for the trees. And to Rachel Huxley and Sophie Kirtley, for your elephantine belief in my book and much trumpeting of it.

To my very first writing friend, Sally Lambert. Thank you for being there as we took our first steps on the journey together, with our fellow critiquers from the Society of Children's Book Writers and Illustrators UMG Herts group: Pauline Simpson, Tony Irving and Sue Prytherch.

To Judi Sissons for your support, and to Gehan de Silva Wijeyeratne for your expert read.

To all my family in Sri Lanka and around the world, and my parents. Love to you all; now please buy the book. A special shout out to my sister, Nihaza, who was with me and the first to know when my agent called to say I was going to be a published author.

Finally and most of all, a special thank you to my little family: Farhaan, Nuha and Sanaa. This book is a love letter to our heritage, wherever in the world we may be.